IT
HAPPENED
TO US

FRANÇOIS HOULE

Dawn Rainbow Books
OTTAWA, ONTARIO

This is a work of fiction. Names, characters, places, and incidents either are a product of the author's imagination or are used fictitiously, and any resemblance to actual people, living or dead, or to businesses, establishments, events, institutions, or locales is completely coincidental.

Copyright © 2015 by François Houle

For permission requests, please email: francois@francoisghoule.com

www.francoisghoule.com

It Happened to Us/François Houle. -- 1st ed.

ISBN: 978-0-9938351-2-4

Published by Dawn Rainbow Books

Cover Design: KD Design

Cover Art: kzenon © 123RF.com

Editor: Ellie Barton

For Colleen and Kayla

Thank you for allowing me to make all the mistakes a husband and father can make and love me regardless. I am truly lucky and blessed.

ONE

March 29, 2012
12:59 p.m.

Mathieu Delacroix stared out the kitchen window into the backyard, something he'd done for years while he washed the dishes or finished a cup of coffee, but today wasn't like any other day. The last time his life had changed this drastically, he was six and disco was all the rage. Now he was forty-one and pretty much listened to whatever radio station his wife or daughter picked. He was dressed in his best black suit, waiting for Lori-Anne to come down. Outside, the grey sky hung low and menacing. Fitting for a late March funeral.

Monday's car accident had changed everything. How could it not? Things like this happened to other people. You heard it on the news but tuned it out. It was easy to dismiss. It wasn't personal.

But this time it was.

The grandfather clock in the living room bonged the hour and he checked his watch. They were running late. His gaze shifted to the enormous bouquet of flowers sitting in a vase on the kitchen table. He couldn't remember who had given it to them. The last three days had been a blur really, a nightmare that made his heart feel like it had been hacked by a butcher. He loosened the knot of his tie but his chest still hurt, his lungs struggling to draw in enough air. He grabbed the edge of the countertop and waited for the moment to pass.

Once it did, Mathieu took a glass from the cupboard and filled it with water. He drank half of it and poured the rest down the drain. In one swift motion, he hurled the glass across the room.

"What happened?" Lori-Anne said from the top of the stairs. "Matt? Is everything all right?"

"Yeah. I dropped a stupid glass."

"Are you cut?"

"No, I'm fine. We should go."

"Be down in a minute. Just need to put my lipstick on."

Mathieu took his jacket off and put it on the back of a chair. Long ago he'd worn suits to work every day, but when Nadia was born he'd traded his dress pants and jackets for work shirts and carpenter's pants. He'd once been a very good copywriter but he'd been happiest staying home to raise his daughter and work in his woodshop. Nothing beat the sweet fragrance of fresh cut oak or mahogany.

Mathieu rolled up his sleeves, took the broom and dustbin from the pantry, swept the debris off the floor and dumped the broken glass into the garbage can. He then stood by the patio door, wondering what he'd do with the massive swing set he'd built fourteen years ago. Nadia had spent afternoons playing on that thing, going up and down the slide, hanging from the monkey bars, asking him to push her higher and higher. At the top of the structure was a small tree house where she'd spent most of her childhood, imagining a boat navigating rough seas, an airplane taking her to faraway places, a spaceship exploring the universe. She hadn't played on it for years and now it just reminded him how quickly life can change.

The phone rang. He stared at it but didn't bother to answer. Probably not for him. The only family he had were his grandparents, and he'd meet up with them at the funeral home.

He glanced at his watch. 1:06 p.m. They really needed to get going. He was about to call Lori-Anne when he heard heels coming down the walnut stairs. She wore a black pant suit and black boots, a matching clutch, no jewelry and no earrings. The only accessory was her two-tone round bracelet watch that she always wore. At forty-three, she was just as striking as when he'd met her twenty years ago. Her hair was shorter now, just down to her shoulders, a golden brown hinting at grey. But it was her piercing light green eyes that weakened him. That, and a laugh he'd always thought of as delicious, sweet, and tasty like dark chocolate.

"You look handsome," she said. "I always liked you in a suit."

"This is one suit I'd rather not be wearing. Who was on the phone?"

"My mom."

"Checking up on us?"

"Worried about us."

They stared at each other for a moment and then Mathieu turned away, swallowing a reply he'd later regret if spoken. He looked out at the silver sky.

"It looks like it might storm," he said.

"I hope it holds until after the service."

The service? He hated that word. It was a funeral, for god's sake. "Rain seems appropriate."

"I'd prefer not to get soaked when we go . . . when we go to the gravesite . . ."

For the first time since the car accident, Lori-Anne lost her composure. She rarely showed that side of herself. Lori-Anne often told Mathieu how hard her father had pushed her so that she, being the youngest and the only girl, would be as tough as her three brothers.

Surprised, Mathieu took a few quick steps around the kitchen table to hold Lori-Anne in his arms. The smell of her perfume reminded him of the backyard's perennial garden he tended during the summer. It was still under a foot of snow.

"Sorry," she said, pulling away. "I'm probably a mess. Let me fix myself."

Mathieu watched her go into the powder room. He wanted a drink – a few shots of whiskey to get through the day. He went to the living room and opened the liquor cabinet. Just a shot. Half a shot. He could feel his breathing get heavier. He forced himself to turn away. To his right, a classic leather sofa showcased dark burgundy carved legs that matched the coffee and end tables, a décor that made the room feel pretentious and stuffy. He rarely spent time here, except when they entertained.

And there hadn't been much of that lately. Lori-Anne worked long hours and he was either in his woodshop or in the den, mindlessly surfing the net. Every now and again he tried to work on the novel he'd started years ago, but his writing had become rusty, his BA in English literature belonging to a past that no longer mattered.

His gaze wandered to the mantel above the fireplace where a picture of Nadia was nestled between an engraved china plate from their wedding and a huge candle that Lori-Anne liked to light in the evenings. Nadia had loved the sweet, wild berry aroma.

Lori-Ann had not lit the candle since the accident.

Mathieu took the picture in his left hand. It shook, just a bit. He stared at the photo as if he could will Nadia back to life. With his right index finger, he traced the contour of his daughter. She was five, top front baby teeth missing, wearing a pink sleeveless vest over a pink long-sleeved shirt. They had walked around Pink Lake in Gatineau Park that day, and Nadia found this huge log camouflaged by coloured leaves. She sat on the fallen tree and flashed him her best smile when he pointed the camera at her.

That toothless grin was a sprinkle of cinnamon over his heart.

Mathieu put the frame back where it belonged on the mantel. He took a step back, the sharp edges of memory raking his gut. His eyes began to sting.

The grandfather clock ticked away, each passing second a mockery. It stood tall and defiant by the archway, too big, its presence overwhelming, like his father-in-law. A wedding gift from Lori-Anne's parents he'd never liked. When they got back from the funeral he would move it to the garage, until he could get GOT-JUNK to come and pick it up.

He'd toss out the furniture too. He could build his own. After all, he was a carpenter and people paid good money for his work. He could see a tall oak bookcase fitting nicely against the far wall, a couple of new picture frames of Nadia to hang on either side. One picture when she was a toddler and then a more recent one, to show the changes over the years. She'd started to look more and more like Lori-Anne, but with his blue-grey eyes. He was probably biased, like any parent, but Nadia had become stunning and he knew that boys must have noticed.

"I'm ready," Lori-Anne said as she came to stand beside him. When she wore heels, they were practically the same height. "What are you thinking?"

Mathieu shrugged. "This room needs a change."

"Really? Why?"

He took a moment. "Reminds me of my great-aunt Florence's living room where kids weren't allowed to go. She might have been my grandfather's older sister, but they were so different."

"I find this room charming, a touch of class inside our modern home," she said. "But we can talk about it later."

"Sure." He glanced at his watch. "We better go."

He locked the front door and they made their way to Lori-Anne's Pathfinder.

"Guess the rain isn't going to wait," she said, feeling a few drops. She climbed into the passenger seat. "Did you bring an umbrella?"

He nodded and started the SUV. "Maybe if we'd gotten rain on Monday instead of snow and freezing pellets, you wouldn't have had that accident."

Lori-Anne turned to stare out the passenger window.

Great! He'd said the wrong thing, again. He wasn't blaming her. It was just a statement he knew to be true, that if it had rained the accident wouldn't have happened because she was a good driver. The word sorry was on the tip of his tongue, but he'd said it so much over the last three days because of their arguing, that it no longer had any meaning.

Mathieu pulled out of the driveway and headed for the funeral home. The silence was uncomfortable so he turned on the radio and was surprised to hear Live 88.5. That was Nadia's radio station, not Lori-Anne's. Their little girl had gone from Justin Bieber to Nirvana disciple in the course of a few months.

And now, she was gone.

TWO

March 29, 2012
1:23 p.m.

L ori-Anne counted the house numbers as they drove by, 58, 60, 62, as if she were seeing her neighbours' homes for the first time in almost fifteen years of living here. A few toddlers were playing in the remaining spring snow while mothers kept a close eye on them, a man in his late fifties was jogging, and a bright yellow Leon's truck was making deliveries. Life moved on so easily, completely unaffected by the death of her daughter. She tried to deny the sadness that made her heart shrivel like a dead rose.

When they'd found out she was pregnant with Nadia after four years of trying and one miscarriage, she and Mathieu had decided living downtown wasn't ideal for raising a child, and the growing community of Bridgehaven where she'd grown up had seemed perfect. Of course, back in the 1970s it had been a boring suburb, seeming so far from everything but really just minutes away from Ottawa. It had been a true bedroom community with a handful of small plazas to provide the basics. Once the size of a small town, the community was now home to nearly 100,000 people and provided all amenities, from schools to big box stores to community centres to medical offices.

Nadia and her cousin Caitlin had grown up together, inseparable like sisters. Lori-Anne's oldest brother, Jim, and his family lived only a few blocks west of them, an easy bike ride.

"Poor Caitlin," Lori-Anne said, the sting of Mathieu's words finally dissipating. "Bad enough that her parents are probably going to get a divorce, and now she loses her cousin."

"Kids are resilient," Mathieu said.

Lori-Anne glared at her husband. "She's fourteen. That's old enough to leave a mark."

"Yeah, I suppose."

"You're not the only one hurting."

"I know," he said with ice in his voice. "I didn't mean it that way."

Lori-Anne rubbed her forehead. Fighting with Mathieu knotted her neck and shoulder muscles, which always led to a pounding headache. It was getting worse, the hostility between them. Everything seemed to set him off, like the world had suddenly turned on him.

"Can you be nice?"

"I'll try."

"Maybe you can to do more than just try."

She stared straight ahead, her lips pressed into a thin line. The rain bounced off the windshield like small pebbles. Monday's snow and ice pellets had sounded just like that. Driving in bad weather had never bothered her, but maybe she'd been distracted by Nadia's behaviour of late, and maybe she'd been driving a little fast, and maybe she didn't see the light turn yellow. She'd wanted to drive her daughter to dance class so they could talk, figure out what was going on, why the attitude.

The conversation didn't go as smoothly as Lori-Anne had rehearsed. She'd tried to make her voice sound casual, like two friends talking about stuff instead of mother and daughter. But Nadia, like all teenagers, was an expert at pushing Lori-Anne's buttons. She could do it without trying.

If she hadn't . . .

Lori-Anne put a hand to her mouth.

Making that phone call to Mathieu had been the hardest thing she'd ever done. She'd wanted to tell him everything, to explain that it wasn't entirely her fault, that the roads were slippery, that it had happened so fast. Sirens, firefighters, paramedics, police officers everywhere. She was shaking so hard she almost dropped her phone. The words were shards of glass in her throat.

"Hey babe," Mathieu said when he answered the phone. "Forget to tell me you love me?"

Her knees had turned to liquid steel. "There's been an accident."

"Are you OK? Is Nadia?"

"I was lucky," she said and felt a blow to the gut. "But . . ."

"Is Nadia OK?"

She heard the panic in his voice and for a moment she wanted to disconnect the call. "No, Matt. She's not OK. I . . . she's . . . she's gone, Matt. Our baby girl is gone. It was awful. I can't get the sound out of my head. She started to scream and then . . . Nadia is dead. Oh God!"

He'd said nothing at first, and then the questions had come too fast. Mostly though, he'd wanted to know why and she'd been unable to give him an answer. Accidents never had reasons. They just happened.

The car slowed and Lori-Anne turned to Mathieu, her eyes filling with fear. This is where their daughter had died, at this intersection. "Why did you come this way?"

"I don't know. Habit."

"Just go."

"The light turned red," he said.

Just to make sure, she looked up at it. A red light would have saved her. But so would paying attention to the road instead of reaching for Nadia's phone. If only her daughter had listened to her, Lori-Anne wouldn't have tried to take that stupid phone away. "You never get a red light when you really need it."

The car inched forward and Lori-Anne watched the intersection until she could no longer see it, like it had faded away. Unfortunately, the crushing of metal and exploding glass and screams would never fade from her memory.

It was her fault.

Why had she been so keen to get Nadia's phone?

Seemed so stupid now.

So what if Nadia was texting while Lori-Anne tried to talk to her? She'd seen Nadia and Caitlin have full conversations with each other while texting other people. It's what teenagers did. Except this time, Lori-Anne had wanted Nadia's full attention, not half, not a quarter, not a tenth. All of it. The past few months she'd gone from good girl to I-don't-like-where-you're-heading sort of girl and Lori-Anne had needed to know why. Something was up and she'd intended to find out because she wasn't the sort of mother who buried her head in the sand and pretended nothing was wrong. When there was a problem, Lori-Anne De-lacroix fixed it.

"Do you think she was doing drugs?"

"What are you talking about?" Mathieu said.

"It would explain a lot."

"It doesn't matter now," he said and slammed his hand on the steering wheel. "She's dead and now we're going to bury her. Drugs aren't a problem anymore."

"Really? You would have let her?"

"Of course not, I would have grounded her sorry little ass, but it no longer matters. Maybe it was something else. Maybe she was having friend trouble."

"We should ask Caitlin."

"It. Doesn't. Matter. Just let it be. Let's remember the Nadia we knew and loved, please. This isn't something we can fix. Our lives are shattered in a million pieces that can't be put back to-gether."

Lori-Anne sat silent. There was something about Monday she hadn't told him yet, words that cut so deep that she felt her heart bleeding on the inside, and now there was no way to ever make it better. She'd never hear Nadia tell her that she hadn't meant to say those words, that they weren't true. The man she'd married would listen to her, would tell her what she wanted to hear, but right now she had no idea where he was and she didn't trust this new Mathieu. To tell him what Nadia had said meant that she'd have to tell him everything, *everything*, that happened leading to the accident, and if she did that she was pretty sure he'd finally have a reason to blame her.

So instead she said the first thing that popped into her head, "What are we going to do about her things?"

"Nothing," he said.

"Maybe Caitlin will want some—"

"No," Mathieu said, leaving no room for compromise.

"It might mean a lot to her. They used to share clothes all the time."

"I said no."

Lori-Anne shifted and pinned him with her eyes. "You'd deny her that?"

"We're not getting rid of her things. We're not donating them. We're not giving them to Caitlin. Everything stays where it is."

"For how long?"

He didn't answer.

"What, are we going to turn her room into some shrine? Is that what you think will get us through this?"

"Maybe."

"No, it won't."

"And you know this how?"

Lori-Anne narrowed her eyes. If she wanted to give Nadia's clothes to Caitlin, then she would. They were of no use to Nadia anymore and Caitlin would love to get them, something to remember Nadia by. No point letting Nadia's things just collect dust and become moldy over time.

"Maybe today isn't the right time for this conversation—"

"Or any other day," he said and took a left onto Greenfield Road. "We're almost at the funeral home and I'd rather not do this in front of your family. No need to give your dad another reason to tell me that I'm unworthy of you."

"He doesn't think that."

"You should see the way he looks at me. He probably wishes you'd never married me."

"Now you're imagining things."

"And you're taking his side."

"I'm not taking any sides, Matt. Let's put this entire conversation away for now."

"Fine." He pulled the car into the funeral home parking lot and found an empty spot near the front. The building was new, modern, with four big white pillars fronting the entrance. "I'm sorry."

Lori-Anne touched his arm. "Me too. We're both stressed."

"I don't want to do this."

"No parent does."

"She's all we had."

"We still have each other. We'll get through this."

"And if we don't?"

Lori-Anne looked at him, her features softening as she remembered their daughter. "Nadia was a beautiful girl who blessed us with fourteen years. Our love for her will get us through this. She will always be with us. That can never be taken from us. Never."

THREE

March 29, 2012
1:44 p.m.

Mathieu watched Lori-Anne rush out to meet her parents and felt more alone than he should. Losing Nadia was something he'd never imagine could happen, and even though he assumed the loss must be just as painful for Lori-Anne, part of him believed that he was suffering more than his wife. The questions that went unanswered were an endless torment that he couldn't run from.

If only he had driven Nadia like he always did. If only he hadn't borrowed the Pathfinder to go get shop supplies. If only the bad weather had held off another hour.

So many factors came into play that day and now nothing could change the outcome.

Mathieu shifted his gaze from Lori-Anne and saw his paternal grandparents, Leon and Flore Delacroix, both in their late eighties, struggling against the wind and rain. He took a breath and stepped out of the Pathfinder. He caught up to his grandmother and took her left arm.

"That's some angry weather," Grandpa said, clamping a fedora on his head.

Mathieu thought it fitted his mood. "How are you feeling, Grandma?"

"Oh, don't worry about me," she said. "I'll manage just fine."

"You're sounding a lot better today," Mathieu said and led them into the funeral home. "How's your arm doing?"

"Probably won't get much better than what it is," she said. "I'm old, and the stroke didn't do me any favours. But your grandpa takes good care of me."

"It's what he's always done best," he said while glancing at his grandfather. "Grandpa's always been good at taking care of us."

He walked his grandparents to the chapel doors at the far end of the lobby. When Mathieu glanced back, he saw Lori-Anne come in with her parents. It didn't take long for her father to spot him and frown. After twenty years, Samuel Weatherly still made Mathieu feel like an outsider, a mistake that should be corrected.

Mathieu turned his attention to his grandparents. "Let me help you to your seats."

"Isn't Lori-Anne coming?" Grandma said.

He took one last look toward his wife, and since she was looking his way he gestured that he was going into the chapel. He saw her nod. "She's just talking to her parents. She'll join us in a minute."

"How is she?" Grandma said.

"Upset," Mathieu said. "She's strong though."

"Something like this," Grandpa said, "can put a lot of stress on a marriage."

Grandma tapped Mathieu's hand. "You and Lori-Anne are going to need each other."

"We're doing okay," he said.

"I can tell a lie when I hear one," Grandpa said.

Mathieu helped his grandmother take a seat in the front row and then turned to his grandfather. "Please Grandpa. I just want to get through the day. Lori-Anne and I will work things out."

"I hope you do," Grandma said. "She's such a lovely girl."

Mathieu stood, watching for Lori-Anne. So many people entered the chapel. Kids from Nadia's school accompanied by parents, teachers he'd met at the last parent-teacher interviews, and a lot of faces he didn't recognize. He accepted condolences, shook hands, muttered thank you.

"Hey Uncle Mathieu," Caitlin said and hugged him. "I can't believe Nad is gone. I miss her so much. Is this really happening?"

Mathieu held her tightly, feeling his niece shake as she sobbed quietly. "Yeah, she's really gone."

"I don't want her to be. What am I going to do without her? She was my best friend."

"I wish none of this was happening too," he said, the words scratching the back of his throat like jagged pieces of broken mirror. "It hardly seems right."

Caitlin cried a bit more and then pulled away, wiping her nose with the back of her hand. Mathieu thought she looked a lot like Nadia, the family resemblance undeniable. The two girls were the same height, same long blond hair. Only their eyes were different, Nadia's had been blue-grey like his while Caitlin's were amber like her mother's.

"Here's your mom with Nicholas and Suzie," he said.

His sister-in-law wrapped her arms around his neck and kissed his cheek. "I'm so so sorry. This is horrible."

"Thanks, Nancy," he said, smelling the booze on her breath. "We'll get through it. Somehow."

"I can't imagine . . ."

"I know," he said.

"Mom," Nicholas said. "Let's get seats."

"I'm sorry," Suzie said and hugged him.

"Thanks," he said to his oldest niece and watched her join the others in the second row.

Finally, Mathieu saw Lori-Anne come in, flanked by her parents and two of her older brothers, Brad and Cory. Brad's wife, Carol, was also there but it looked like they'd left the kids back in Vancouver. Mathieu noticed that Jim, Nancy's husband, was nowhere to be seen. That was so like him not to show up.

By now seats were scarce and people stood along the sides and at the back. Mathieu watched Lori-Anne lead her family up the middle aisle, people going quiet as they walked by. Lori-Anne came to stand beside him while everyone else took seats beside Nancy except for his mother-in-law, Victoria, who came to hug him.

"My dearest condolences, Mathieu."

"Thank you."

"Such a shame," she said, letting him go and wiping her nose with a used tissue she held in her right hand. "I loved that little bird."

"Little bird?"

"When she was a baby, she'd purse her lips when I fed her. It reminded me of a little bird's peak."

Mathieu couldn't find the strength to smile.

"We'll get through this," Victoria said before taking a seat beside her husband.

"Lots of people," Lori-Anne said into Mathieu's ear. "You never realize the impact someone has in other people's lives."

"She wasn't just ours anymore," he said and glanced around. People tried to avert their gaze, but not before he saw pity in their eyes.

He looked away. He didn't want their pity. He wanted his daughter.

"Why?" he said, possibly for the hundredth time. "She had so much ahead of her. We had so much ahead of us. We'll never be grandparents."

Tears streamed down Lori-Anne's face. He had no words of comfort, just this raw anger deep in his core wanting to lay waste to everything in its path. If only he could smash something, anything, everything, maybe he'd find some relief.

A door opened and Mathieu looked up.

Father Russo stood before them, his arms raised in blessing. The congregation went silent. And then stifled sobs started way in the back and rose like a wave toward the front. Behind him, Mathieu heard Caitlin crying loudly while Nancy tried to soothe her. His grandmother also began to cry and Mathieu took her hand.

"We have gathered here today to pay our respect . . ." Father Russo said but Mathieu had tuned him out. He stared at the life-sized crucifix that hung on the back wall, and felt little comfort in seeing Jesus hanging from it. How could God, who allowed that to happen to His son, care about what happened to Mathieu's daughter?

No answers came.

ᙏ ᙓ

Father Russo spoke fondly of Nadia, bringing her back to life, if only in select memories. Lori-Anne had met with him the day before to go over the ceremony, and had supplied the details that personalized her daughter.

She sat there remembering when things were much simpler and happier, when Nadia was a toddler playing with her toys in the living room while she prepared Sunday night dinner. Sunday afternoons had always been hers and Nadia's as Mathieu took care of the outside, mowing the lawn, trimming the shrubs, washing the cars, and occasionally playing a round of golf with her brother Cory. A routine she now realized had been privileged harmony.

Lori-Anne took her husband's hand and laced her fingers with his. It felt good to be touching him, an act of intimacy that had eluded them since the accident. She quickly glanced at Mathieu and doubt squeezed her heart when she saw the agony in his eyes. Today was hard, but she knew what to expect. She had no idea what was to come for them after today. A distance had settled between them that had never been there before and she didn't know what it meant. They'd had a wonderful marriage, a close and loving relationship. He'd always been the man she'd wanted and needed, and she'd never imagined that that would change. She'd also never imagined that her daughter would die.

Father Russo finished and looked her way.

"Come," Lori-Anne said.

"Where?"

"To the front."

"Why?"

"So people can express their condolences."

"OK."

Lori-Anne stood, still holding Mathieu's hand, and he followed. Nadia's urn, and an 8x10 framed picture taken this past Christmas showing Nadia wearing a new black-and-cream sweater with a pair of skinny jeans, sat on a pedestal. A beautiful flower arrangement filled the entire area around the base.

Lori-Anne took a deep breath and faced the gathering, Mathieu at her side.

At Father Russo's invitation, people began to move toward the front.

C3 80

Mathieu shook hands and accepted hugs from people he didn't know. At first, he tried to stay in the moment, but soon his thoughts turned to cherished memories.

He recalled the day he'd brought Nadia home from the hospital, a bundle of life, squirming and cooing. The sweetest sounds he'd ever heard. Her tiny fingers grabbing his nose when he snuggled against her belly.

How he wanted to hold her, touch her, kiss her one more time. He wanted to be angry with her, yell at her, ground her. He wanted to sneak into her room after she'd fallen asleep and watch her sleep for a moment, knowing that he was the luckiest man alive. Most of all, he wanted to tell her how much he loved her.

He shook hands with Brad and hugged Carol.

"Thanks for making the long trip to be here," he said.

"Wish it was for better circumstances," Brad said.

Mathieu nodded.

Next came Cory. His gay brother-in-law. They hugged. He'd always liked Cory. He was the black sheep in the family so it made him an instant ally against Samuel.

"If you need anything," Cory said. "Let me know."

"Thanks."

The line of people never seemed to end but in a way it was a good thing, showed that Nadia had mattered. Still, it was hard to accept the same condolences over and over again as if he was hearing them for the first time. Unfortunately, there wasn't much else people could say.

☙ ❧

Once everyone had expressed their sympathy and exited the chapel, it became too quiet. Lori-Anne turned to Mathieu and rubbed his arm. "How are you?"

"Hanging in. You?"

They stood in front of Nadia's urn.

"I'll be fine," she said.

"She looks so pretty in that picture."

"We almost had to take her phone away so she'd get dressed to go to my parents' house."

"She wanted to play with her new phone. What teenager wouldn't?"

"I know," she said. "I'm so glad we managed to get this photo."

"Me too."

"We were good parents, weren't we?"

"I like to think so."

They stood for a moment longer, the missing presence in their lives becoming more and more real and Lori-Anne's urge to deny its existence a growing lump deep inside of her. She would never get the chance to make amends for what had happened, for what had been said. She wanted to make peace with Nadia, but it felt rather one-sided and unfinished.

"We should get going," she said, her chest feeling so small she had to force herself to breathe. "Do you want to carry the urn?"

"Sure."

Lori-Anne followed Mathieu down the middle aisle, but before exiting the chapel she turned and looked at Nadia's picture.

I'm sorry, she mouthed.

CƆ ꝏ

Mathieu felt the dampness in the air the moment he stepped out of the funeral home. The rain had changed to a drizzle. The parking lot had emptied quickly and only family remained.

"Why do we need a hearse?" he said.

"It's part of the service," Lori-Anne said.

Mathieu made his way to the hearse and handed the urn to the driver. The man secured his daughter's remains and closed the door.

"We'll follow," he said to the driver. "Close."

Lori-Anne was already in the car waiting for him. He started the engine and shivered, a chill in his bones. The drizzle on the windshield made everything blurry so he set the wipers to the intermittent setting.

He glanced at Lori-Anne. "Is any of this real?"

She shook her head. "I keep hoping it's not."

He followed the hearse out of the parking lot, and his family pulled in line behind him. At the first set of lights, they stopped. People rushed across the intersection, their heads bowed under umbrellas. No one seemed to notice the hearse. No one knew or cared that a young girl had ceased to breathe, ceased to exist, ceased to matter. Mathieu wanted to roll down the window and shout, *It's my daughter in there.*

He rubbed his face with a callused hand.

The light turned green and they moved on. The developed neighbourhood gave way to farmland. They rode in silence. Ten minutes later they turned into the cemetery.

ɔȝ ʚɔ

Lori-Anne slid out of the car and took a few hesitant steps toward her husband. He was leaning against the hood, his hands shoved in the pockets of his overcoat, his head bent down as if pressed by an unbearable weight.

She was sure all the grey in his hair had showed up overnight.

Behind them car doors slammed shut and footsteps crunched stones. Monday's snow was almost gone, washed away by today's rain. The grass wasn't visible yet, but another wet day might do it.

"Are you going to get her?"

"Yeah," Mathieu said. "I was just thinking . . ."

"I know."

She watched Mathieu take the urn from the driver. When he faced her, tears streaked down his face, matching hers.

She went to him.

They held each other, Nadia between them.

❀

Mathieu and Lori-Anne stood inches from the gravesite, their family forming a semicircle around them. Father Russo finished with the Lord's Prayer and invited Mathieu to put his daughter to rest.

He went down on one knee, kissed the urn, and carefully set Nadia's remains. He took a handful of dirt that had been left beside the small hole that had been dug for the urn and let it trickle through his fingers.

"Goodbye, sweetie," he said.

Mathieu got up and stood by his wife. His grandmother, to his left, rubbed his arm. He looked at his grandfather and saw the same sadness in the old man's eyes that he felt in his heart. No one said anything as they took turns letting a handful of dirt cover the urn before walking away.

The afternoon was getting late and a northerly wind picked up, biting at his face and moving the steel-coloured sky above. Mathieu looked up and noticed the pale shadow of the moon between cloud breaks.

Goodnight Moon.

How many times had he read that book to her at bedtime? By the time Nadia was three, she could recite the words as he read them. To this day, he remembered most of them too. He recalled how she would hang on, not giving in to sleep until he'd read the last syllable. Then she would close her eyes and cuddle with her teddy and blanket, a smile on her face. He would lean over and kiss her forehead, and she'd fall asleep within seconds.

He didn't know why he'd just thought of that, except that bedtime had been one of his favourite moments, a perfect way to end the day. Mathieu closed his eyes and let the memory wrap itself around him, the comfort it brought like slipping into a warm bed.

When he opened his eyes, the moon was gone and so was the life he'd loved.

Mathieu looked at his parents' gravestones, a few feet away in the family plot. In the past year he'd only come twice to visit them, the years erasing any memory he'd had of them long ago, but now he needed them more than ever.

Mom, Dad, take care of your granddaughter.

FOUR

April 2, 2012
7:55 a.m.

L ori-Anne stepped out of the elevator and walked with purpose toward her office at the far end of the eighth floor. She nodded to people who said hi or offered condolences but after the fifth *thank you* her throat started to contract and dry up, the words barely audible even to her ears, and she now second-guessed her decision to come back today. No one expected to see her so soon and the surprised looks, or maybe they were disbelieving looks, confirmed this. It was all she could do not to run the last twenty feet to her office and lock herself in until everyone left at five.

Nadia's absence at home had been too obvious and she'd thought that maybe here, where her daughter never came, she could forget the hole in her soul for a while.

Lori-Anne shut the door and put her briefcase on the expansive oak desk. She took a deep breath to slow her pounding heart and walked to the wall of windows that looked down Elgin Street, City Hall, and Confederation Park to the left. During Winterlude festivities each February, the three of them always went down to admire the ice sculptures carved by artists from around the world who came to showcase their talents, and then they'd skate on the Rideau Canal.

Normally, she never tired of the view.

But today wasn't a normal day no matter how much she'd tried to deny it. And the people rushing about in a steady stream of activity told another story, driving home that nothing had really been changed by the death of her daughter, that for most people it was just another busy Monday. That reality left her short of breath and light headed. She collapsed into her expensive high-backed leather chair, her head in her hands.

Nadia's death means nothing to anyone else.

The morning conversation with Mathieu slammed her back in her chair.

"I need to do this," she said.

"Why? Our daughter just died. I think taking a few days, a week, is what normal people do. Your work can wait."

"I know it can wait," she said while selecting an outfit. "But maybe I can't stay here all day. I need to do something to keep my mind occupied."

"You can't run away."

"That's not what I'm doing."

"Really?"

"Yes, really. Maybe you should get out of bed and do something too. You've lain around all weekend."

"What do you want me to do? Our daughter is dead. I really don't feel like doing anything. I can't simply move on as if nothing happened."

"It's not what I'm doing."

"Sure looks it to me."

Lori-Anne picked one of her pant-suits, light grey, and an off-white silk blouse.

"That must be some important meeting. And you've picked your most expensive suit, too."

Lori-Anne stopped buttoning her blouse. "I don't have any important meetings, as far as I know. I almost always wear this suit on Mondays."

"Why?"

She shrugged. "Habit."

They stared at each other. For a second she questioned going to work, but being stuck at home with Mathieu and his moods would be worse. The drift between them, the hostility, was growing. He'd become cold, at times said words that were hurtful, and hadn't touched her since the funeral.

A knock at her door brought her back to the present. Her assistant, Sara, stepped in holding a large cup.

"Here's your coffee."

"You're a life saver," Lori-Anne said and took a sip. "Anything I should know?"

Sara just stood there, glassy-eyed. "I'm so sorry for your loss. I mean, I know I told you this at the service, which was beautiful by the way . . . oh God, that probably sounds awful."

"Thank you," she said. "I was glad to see you and so many others. Mathieu and I really appreciated it. It's certainly not an easy time for us."

"OK, well . . . huh, let me know if you need anything. Andy isn't in yet but I'm sure he'll come and talk to you since you're here. And I cleared your calendar since I thought you'd take a few days."

"I didn't know what else to do. I thought maybe if I kept busy, it would help somehow."

Sara left and Lori-Anne powered her laptop. Once it was up she tackled the two hundred plus emails that had landed in her inbox over the past week. Before they'd installed the spam filter it probably would have been close to five hundred emails, most of them offering Viagra at incredible prices or some sort of annoying porn. About halfway through the chore her enthusiasm waned and something to her left caught her eye.

Nadia's grade six graduation picture.

She rubbed her forehead. A moment, that's all she needed. But it wasn't. She reached for the picture and stared at it, her chest feeling so tight her heart wanted to tear it apart. She picked up the phone but slammed it back down. What would she say to Mathieu? *Hey you were right. This was a bad idea. Should have listened to you.*

Instead Lori-Anne put the picture face down on her desk.

After a few minutes, she regained some control and plowed through the rest of her emails, giving them a quick look over and deleting as many as she could. A few she moved to her important folder to look at later. An hour had slipped by when Andy entered her office without knocking.

"Why're you here?"

She sat back in her chair. "Don't I work here?"

He sat on the corner of her desk. "You know that's not what I asked. You lost your daughter. I expected you to take some time off. As much as you need. Maybe I should send you home."

"I'll be fine."

"You sure?"

"I'm sure," she said.

"Last chance."

"Andy."

"OK then. Meeting at ten. We'll go over the Green Solution account."

"Sounds good."

"I'd like to know where we're at before we meet with them Thursday."

"No problem."

Now Lori-Anne had focus, something she knew would occupy her mind for a few hours. When she returned from the washroom, there was a fresh cup of coffee on her desk. She pulled the Green Solution file and got busy.

At 9:50, Sara stuck her head in the office and whispered, "Nancy is on the phone."

"I have a few minutes. Put it through."

"OK."

"Hey Nance, what's up?"

"What are you doing at work?" Nancy said. "I called to see how you guys were doing and Mathieu told me you went to work. I didn't believe him at first but then he kept saying you weren't home. So, there you are."

"I know it seems strange, but I needed to."

"Are you OK?"

"I had a weak moment earlier, but I've settled."

"I wish I had your resolve."

"Not so sure I have any," Lori-Anne said. "Can I confide in you?"

"You know you can."

"Things aren't great with Mathieu. The tension between us is awful and to be honest, I wanted to get away from him as much as I didn't want to be home missing my daughter."

"He's hurting. I'm sure it'll blow over and you guys will work it out. I mean, what you two are going through, it makes my problem seem so meaningless."

"Your troubled marriage isn't meaningless." Lori-Anne thought she heard ice cubes in a glass. "You and Jim, any chance of fixing things?"

"You'd have to ask him. Your dear brother hasn't been around lately. If I had to guess, I'd say we're pretty much over. Twenty-seven years of marriage kaput."

"Oh Nancy, you're sure you can't work it out?"

"Takes two to tango, they say, and I'm all alone on the dance floor."

"I'm sorry."

"Me too. You know, your brother is the only man I've ever been with. Stole my heart in high school, stole my best years, and now he's trading me for a younger model."

Sara came in and pointed to her watch. "I wish I could talk longer but I have to run to a meeting. How about I call you later?"

Sucking on ice cube sound. "Sure. We can both cry about our shitty lives."

"It'll get better."

"Doubt it."

"I got to go."

Lori-Anne hung up, grabbed her file, and rushed to the meeting room, Nancy's cynical outlook on the state of their lives trailing her down the hall.

ଔ ଓ

The meeting lasted through lunch and by 1:30 Lori-Anne was famished. She went down to the food court on the ground floor, bought a chicken salad with a Diet Coke, and found a table. Thoughts of Nancy came to her. She was worried. Nancy had never been much of a drinker, but that had changed.

She recalled Caitlin mentioning something about her parents at Christmas but Lori-Anne hadn't really paid attention, or hadn't wanted to believe it. Her oldest brother had never been her favourite, sharp around the edges like her dad, but as far as she knew he'd always been faithful.

Not anymore.

Now she understood why Caitlin had been around more than usual. Hanging out at their house had been better than going home and dealing with whatever nonsense was happening there. Lori-Anne grabbed her cell and called Nancy.

"Sorry I had to cut you off earlier."

"I understand."

"Are you OK? You don't sound right."

"I'm fine," she said, stretching the last syllable. "Just having a little cocktail."

"That's not like you."

"Well, you know, my husband is screwing someone else behind my back."

"I know," Lori-Anne said. "I'd like to wring his neck."

"He didn't even come to his niece's funeral. Who forgets something like that?"

Lori-Anne had wondered the same thing but had decided not to bother with Jim. Most of their conversations ended in ugly disagreement. Mostly because he knew that if she wanted it, their father would make her president of Weatherly Construction. But she didn't want it.

"I'm concerned about you."

"And I'm concerned about you and Mathieu. I'm only losing a marriage. If I lost one of the kids—I don't know what I'd do. Please tell me everything is fine between you two."

"Everything is fine." No need to burden Nancy, she was such a sweet and wonderful woman. "It will be in time, I'm sure."

"If you need anything at all."

"I'll be sure to ask. There's one thing you can do for me."

"Absolutely."

"Don't drink yourself into a stupor, please. My idiot brother isn't worth it." She heard Nancy sob. "You're a good person. You raised four great kids."

"Thank you," Nancy said through tears. "Maybe there's a reason Derek works way up north. He probably figured out when he was young to stay away from his dad."

"Does he know?"

"I'm sure one of the kids probably told him. They keep in touch with Facebook and texting. Can you believe he'll be twenty-six on April 29?"

"Makes us seem old."

"Doesn't it?"

"I think we both need to keep our heads up. It's going to get better."

"I sure hope so," Nancy said. "I keep thinking, what did I do wrong? You know? Why isn't he happy with me? It hurts."

"Don't blame yourself. He's the one cheating."

"I know but—"

"I'm there for you and the kids. Maybe I should call my brother and—."

"Please don't," Nancy said, her voice regaining strength. "You and Matt have enough to deal with. I just have to figure out what's right for me and the kids. I should let you get back to work."

"We'll talk soon."

Lori-Anne dumped her empty salad container and pop can in the recycling bin and headed back to her office. She wanted to phone Mathieu but wasn't sure how that conversation would fare. She didn't want to get in a fight with him, or get all upset over Nadia. But they needed to talk before their marriage went the way of Nancy and Jim's. Relationships failed every day for petty reasons, but there was nothing petty about losing a child. Somehow, she and Mathieu had to find a way to get through this together, not alone. They each had their own grief, but she wanted to share hers and wanted him to share his. That's the only way they were going to survive this tragedy. After all these years, her love for him was just as strong, and she hoped his was too. She'd give anything to have Nadia back, but she was gone and it was just the two of them now, like when they'd first met. But it wasn't like that anymore. They weren't young and innocent and full of silly hopes. Hadn't seemed silly back then, maybe a little optimistic or romantically hopeful, but that's what being young was all about. Now they were middle-aged and a bit beaten.

Lori-Anne picked up Nadia's picture and held it in her hands. Then she placed it in the middle drawer of her desk. Right now it was just too painful to look at, that beautiful smiling face begging to be touched. She hoped tomorrow, or the day after that, she'd be better and could bring the picture out again.

Seven months would go by before she did, and things would be a lot worse than she ever could have imagined they could get.

FIVE

Mathieu woke up disoriented, and then realized he'd fallen asleep on the recliner in the spare bedroom. He'd converted it to an office long ago, when he and Lori-Anne had come to terms with the fact that they wouldn't have any more kids. Two miscarriages after Nadia and then nothing for several years had been disappointing. At least they'd been able to have Nadia.

Mathieu looked at his watch. Just after midnight. He got up and walked down the dark hallway, bypassing his bedroom and going into Nadia's. Over the past week, every night, he got up two or three times and went to his daughter's room, hoping that everything that had happened over the last couple of weeks was just a nightmare. It wasn't. Nadia was really gone.

His heart sank a little deeper inside his chest. He dropped onto her bed and grabbed one of her toy animals, *stuffies* she'd called them since she was two. She had so many that they covered half the bed and even at fourteen, she wouldn't get rid of them.

He stared at the frog in his hands. Where had it come from? He couldn't remember. Some he'd bought. Others she'd gotten from family. And some were won at fairs they'd gone to over the years. It didn't matter.

A sliver of light knifed through the small gap between the curtains. Mathieu walked over to the window and peeked out. The moon, almost full, hung low and bright in the sky. Nadia's room looked out the front of the house, at the big red maple tree. The road was quiet, the neighbourhood tucked in for the night.

Mathieu didn't think he'd be able to fall asleep for a while. He put the frog on the bed and walked out, making sure to close the door. Back in his office, he looked at pictures of Nadia's childhood on his computer. He'd bought his first digital camera when she was four, and he'd taken thousands of photos over the past ten years. Photo albums of when she was a baby filled the bookcase beside his desk.

Click.

A picture of Nadia dressed as Hermione, when she was six. The movie *Harry Potter and the Prisoner of Azkaban* had been the craze that summer and she'd wanted that costume for Halloween.

A sickly feeling dropped like cold metal into the pit of his stomach.

Click.

Nadia and Caitlin playing outside on the swing set that same autumn. For the first time since the funeral, he wondered how Caitlin was doing. She hadn't been around, and that felt strange. She'd always come home after school with Nadia, the two of them raiding the fridge before heading up to Nadia's room.

Click.

Nadia making a snow angel in the first snow of winter. The metal in his gut seemed to grow heavier. But he couldn't stop himself.

Click.

"What are you doing?"

He jumped. "I couldn't sleep. Why are you up?"

"I woke up and you weren't in bed, again," Lori-Anne said. "Maybe you should take a Nytol before bed."

"You know how I feel about pills."

"But if you can't sleep at night."

He shook his head. "I'm fine."

"You're not," she said. "I'd really like you to see a doctor."

"I don't need a doctor for a few sleepless nights," he said.

"Maybe not," she said, taking a step into his office. "But you might need help for your mood."

"I'm. Fine."

"Did you hear your tone right now?"

He said nothing.

"Matt, you're getting moodier each day. All you do is sit in that chair and look at her pictures. I just don't think that's healthy."

"Why do we take pictures if we're never going to look at them?"

"We look at pictures for fun, to laugh and remember the good times. You should see your face when you're looking at her pictures. You're like transfixed . . . and pained."

"I can't let her go like you have."

Lori-Anne stared down at him. "You think it's that easy for me?"

"Didn't stop you from going back to work. You're right back on schedule, like nothing happened."

"I have a job to do."

"Our daughter died," he said, slapping his hand on the desk. "We buried her last Thursday and Monday you were back at work. Doesn't that seem wrong to you?"

Lori-Anne folded her arms across her chest. "I thought it would help if I kept busy. You're not the only one hurting and there's times when . . ."

They stared at each other.

"I think you should have stayed home," he said.

"So we can do this all day long? Maybe I wanted to get away from our fighting." Lori-Anne turned to leave.

"Most people wouldn't go back to work so soon. I haven't worked on any of my orders this week."

She whipped around. "Maybe you should, it would occupy your mind."

"The last thing I want to do is use power tools when I can't concentrate. A bad combo."

"I get that," Lori-Anne said. "But you can't lie in bed all day or look at pictures. Your clients will expect their orders."

"I was able to reschedule them. A couple cancelled and I'll refund their deposits." He suddenly felt drained. "It's killing me inside. All I ever wanted was a family, to have a few kids, and the only one we had is gone. I'm just so angry."

"I am too . . ."

Mathieu pointed at his laptop. "Looking at her pictures gets me through the day. I keep hoping that tomorrow I'll feel better, but I don't. It's like my insides are one big tangled mess of rage that I can't get rid of. It suffocates me. I can't think clearly. There's times when I don't think I can take another breath, the panic rolling over me like a tank. I'm afraid of forgetting her so I look at her pictures and I remember how happy we were, but that ache in me never goes away. It just never goes away."

"Why don't you see your doctor? Maybe you need something to help you for now, until you do feel better."

"I can't."

"You're so stubborn. You'd rather feel like that than get help?"

He shook his head. "It's Good Friday. Offices are closed."

"Then call Monday."

"I'll think about it," he said.

SIX

L ori-Anne lay in bed, alone, listening to heaven's tears knock at her window. The rain sounded like tiny fists against the glass, tiny fists of children wanting to come in, the children she'd not been able to conceive. She'd always felt blessed that at least they'd had Nadia, that for some reason, they'd been allowed to have her.

However short that time had been.

And it had been way too short. She missed her daughter, the feel of carrying her when she was pregnant, holding that tiny baby for the first time, giving her her first bath. Mathieu had stayed home with Nadia but Lori-Anne had had wonderful times with her daughter too. Going shopping with her every August to buy going-back-to-school clothes, helping with homework, showing her how to apply makeup just last year so she wouldn't look like a hooker.

The tiny smile on her lips faded quickly.

So now what? If Nadia was gone, was she still a mother? She wanted to believe that she was, but to whom? Nadia's spirit? Nadia's memory? That didn't seem like much. Maybe bordered on the not-right-of-mind sort of personality. Mathieu's the one who had showed those signs, not her. No, she'd done her best to pick up the pieces and move forward, not move on because that sounded cold, like denying anything bad had happened. Moving forward encompassed everything that had happened, and brought it along. Nothing was left behind.

The difference was subtle, if it existed at all. She knew that. Whereas her husband had buried himself in a past that no longer was, she moved forward to a future that hopefully would return them to serenity, and maybe someday to subdued happiness.

That hope fuelled her to keep trying.

But it was hard. She hadn't handled the past month very well. The man she loved had become a broken soul she couldn't reach. Her life was out of control and the worst part was that she blamed herself. All she'd wanted to do was to talk with Nadia, but instead they'd started to argue and things had gone horribly wrong.

What had she expected? Nadia had been an emotional mess, confused and angry at the world, at her parents. *You guys don't get me, you don't let me do anything, you're such dinosaurs.* Lori-Anne had heard that plenty of times. The same old thing in the car—Nadia complaining and texting, ignoring her. On top of that, Lori-Anne's Blackberry kept vibrating, someone from work trying to reach her no doubt.

That day was better left alone. Nothing could change what happened.

Mother's Day. Maybe she should just hide in her bedroom all day, wait it out. She was pretty sure Mathieu wouldn't bother her if she didn't come out. It could be that easy. Just lay low for the day, sleep, wait it out.

She got up.

Lori-Anne Delacroix wasn't the type of woman who gave up, who hid from life. So what if it was Mother's Day and there was no one to call her mom anymore. She still had a mother and if Mathieu didn't want to accompany her, she'd go spend the day at her parents and treat her mom to a wonderful day.

Yes, that's what she'd do. She headed for the bathroom to shower and caught her reflection in the mirror. There were dark circles under her eyes, and maybe a few grey hairs. The woman staring back, it wasn't her. Lori-Anne turned away from the mirror, unable to face Nadia's killer. Maybe she was being harsh, but if she'd paid attention to the road, if she hadn't been so determined to get Nadia's phone away from her, if Nadia had been listening, then maybe her daughter would still be here, sleeping in her bed where she belonged.

If only, if only, if only.

Their lives would be as they'd always been, pleasant and uneventful. Ordinary, but that was fine. Better than fine. Ordinary was fantastic. Lori-Anne would rather be dealing with an ordinary, sullen, and impenetrable teenager than to be sucked into the hole left by her absence. That absence widened the distance between her and Mathieu, every day finding them a little further away from each other. Lori-Anne didn't really know what to do. Mathieu didn't want to talk. When she tried, he would get angry and at times mean, saying things she couldn't believe came from the man she loved. Their conversations were like a mine field. A wrong word, a wrong gesture, a wrong look could set him off.

Last week, she'd searched the three medicine cabinets, his office, even his woodshop. She hadn't found a prescription. He'd never gone to see his doctor. He wasn't getting better. They weren't getting better.

If only, if only, if only.

Lori-Anne got in the shower and let the hot water cascade over her, the tension in her neck and back easing a bit. She dressed in jeans and a pink t-shirt, and made her way down to the kitchen where nothing special waited for her.

慙 慘

Mathieu was in the garage, trying his best to finish a dresser that was due this coming week. He'd put the job off as long as he could, and it wouldn't be perfect. The flaws would have bothered him in the past, but he was out of time and he doubted his client would see them. This dresser had been a real struggle, his love for woodworking simply not there, a chore instead of a passion. His next project, a bed for a little girl, would be even harder to do. It was the same plan he'd used for Nadia's bed. A couple of times he'd picked up the phone to call and tell the client he couldn't do it, but he'd already pushed back the date and the client had been so understanding. Besides, Mathieu didn't think it would be right to deny the little girl a new bed just because of his own problems.

"Shit," he said as he sliced the tip of his index finger with a freshly sharpened chisel. He headed for the powder room and stuck his finger under cold water.

His grandfather's warnings ran through his head. *Woodworkers lose fingers every day because they're not concentrating.* Lucky he hadn't been using the table saw.

Mathieu spread Polysporin on the wound and wrapped the cut with a bandage he found in the medicine cabinet. He popped two Tylenol in his mouth to ease the sting. Some pains were a lot easier to deal with. Even his right knee, the one he'd torn playing hockey when he was sixteen, was easier to handle than the never-ending ache he felt in his heart all day long. He splashed water on his face and suddenly grabbed the sides of the sink.

Nadia. As plain as day. It happened all the time when he closed his eyes. He could almost touch her, but he knew if he tried, she would run through his fingers like water from the faucet.

Mathieu opened his eyes and turned the faucet off. When he straightened, he didn't like what he saw in the mirror. He couldn't remember the last time he'd been able to see his cheekbones so predominantly, and his eyes were bloodshot and lifeless. The couch wasn't exactly comfortable. But he couldn't share the bed with Lori-Anne. When he looked at her, he saw Nadia. When he smelled her, he smelled Nadia.

The phone rang.

Mathieu rushed to the kitchen and checked the call display.

"Hey Grandpa?" he said.

"How are you?"

"Sliced my finger with a chisel," he said, knowing this wasn't what his grandfather was really asking him. "Should've been paying attention."

"I don't need to remind you."

"The chisel reminded me."

Grandpa chuckled. "I guess it did."

"How's Grandma?"

"She's having a pretty good morning," Grandpa said. "But she's worried about you."

Mathieu looked at the clock on the stove. It was just after 9:30. He thought it would be later. He couldn't remember when he'd gone to work in the shop.

"Me?"

"You know your grandmother."

A wonderful woman. Raised and cared for him when her rearing days should have been long done. He'd been difficult at first and she'd known how to soothe his sadness. Night after night, he'd wake up screaming, asking for his mommy and daddy, and when grandma came rushing to comfort him, he'd kick and scream that he didn't want her, he wanted his parents. Grandma never got angry with him, never raised her voice, never walked away. She'd stay with him until he fell back to sleep. He couldn't remember how many months that had lasted, but he was so grateful now for the love and patience that she'd given him. She was not just a grandmother, but a mother as well.

"Tell her I'm fine," he said. "I'm fine."

"You know I don't believe you," Grandpa said. "And I'm not going to lie to your grandmother. We're both worried about you and Lori-Anne. How are you two getting on?"

Mathieu ran a hand across his chin. Every morning, he got up, hopeful, meaning to talk with her, spend time with her, but his anger always took over. One second everything was fine and then rage would rip through him like a tornado.

"It's been tense."

"Maybe counselling would help."

"You don't strike me as believing in that sort of thing. Is that Grandma's idea?"

"We've discussed it. Your grandmother and I did see someone when your parents died. It was difficult opening up to a stranger, but in time it became easier. It did help us. Besides, we had you to think about."

Mathieu looked around the kitchen. It was so neat, clean. Nadia would leave the bread on the counter, crumbs scattered about, a dirty knife beside the peanut butter container left beside the toaster, her empty cup forgotten on the table. But now the kitchen was spotless, like no one used it. Mathieu was home alone all day and Lori-Anne worked passed dinner time most days. Who was he supposed to take care of? It was like he lived alone.

"Yeah, well. We don't have anyone to worry about."

"But you do," Grandpa said. "You have a wife to care for and she has a husband."

Mathieu didn't know what to say.

"Listen," Grandpa said. "Why don't the two of you come on over for lunch? You and I can make something special for Mother's Day."

"I don't think Lori-Anne wants to be reminded of what she's missing," Mathieu said. "It would be too hard on her."

"On her," Grandpa said, "or on you?"

"Both, I guess."

"Get back on the horse, son," Grandpa said. "You need to get back to living."

"Grandpa, it's not that easy or that simple."

"Of course it's not," Grandpa said. "Life isn't easy. Marriage isn't easy. Nothing worthwhile is easy. But what's the alternative? Things happen and we suffer through it and we find the courage to move on, hopefully stronger than before. What happened is a real shame, but life goes on. You have a wife who loves you. Use that love to find your courage."

Mathieu stood by the kitchen sink, staring out the window at the old play structure. *Push me higher Daddy, higher.* Nadia's giggles filled the backyard while Lori-Anne sunbathed on a lounge chair. A shot of happiness and longing ran through his veins.

"I'll have to ask Lori-Anne when she gets up," Mathieu finally said.

"Okay, you do that, and call back."

"Sure Grandpa."

Mathieu put the phone down and heard Lori-Anne step into the kitchen. He saw something in her eyes, like she'd hoped for something but now had to settle for disappointment.

"I thought you were still in bed."

"Showered and dressed," she said. "Who was on the phone?"

"My grandparents invited us over for lunch," he said. "We should probably go considering it's Mother's—"

He caught himself but not before he saw Lori-Anne's disappointment turn into something deeper and sadder, a burden crushing her spirit.

"I didn't know what to do about today."

"I'm fine," she said and moved toward the coffee machine.

"Let me make that," he said. "I woke up early and just went straight to work and didn't even think of making coffee."

"Or anything," she said.

"I'm sorry," he said. "I'll make us something."

She shook her head. "Don't worry about it." She filled the coffee machine with water and coffee grind and pushed the AUTO button. Percolating coffee broke the silence.

"Damn it, Lori-Anne," he said. "I'm trying to be nice."

"You shouldn't have to try," she said.

"Look," he said. "No matter what I did today, there was no way to be right, so I did nothing. But that's also wrong. Nadia's gone either way."

"I know," she said, her voice weak. "I don't think it's really about today. It's about the last seven weeks. You've been somewhere else. I can't talk to you. You've shut me out."

"I've shut you out? You're always working."

"Why would I want to be here?"

"So it's all my fault?"

"Mathieu, will you go see your doctor? Maybe he can prescribe something that will help your moods and your grief, and then maybe we'll have a chance to make things better between us."

"I'm fine," he said. "I'm not going on any stupid medication."

Lori-Anne extended her hand as if to touch him, but then pulled it back. "Only for a little while, until you get passed this."

"Are you going on medication?"

"I'm not the one who's depressed," she said.

"Are you sure about that?"

"I'm still functioning. I get up and go to work every day and I don't bite anyone's head off. I can't say the same about you."

"I get my work done," he said.

"Do you? I haven't seen any finished projects since before the accident. Aren't people going to start demanding the furniture they've ordered?"

"That's my problem."

"Sure. Fine," she said.

"Anyway, I'm just finishing a dresser so I'm getting things done."

"Okay." She took a cup from the cupboard and filled it with coffee. "I still think you should see your doctor."

He filled his own cup. "I don't see how that's going to help. I don't believe in that stuff."

"Depression is a chemical imbalance. Severe trauma, stress caused by loss can trigger it. There's some good medication out there that can help."

"What, you're a doctor now?"

"I did some research and you have all the signs. There's no harm in trying. Please, if not for you then for us. We can't live like this."

He put his cup down on the counter. "I miss her. So, damn, much."

"And so do I."

"But you weren't the one here with her every day, raising her, watching her grow. I scheduled my days around her. It was the best feeling in the world. Now that she's gone, it's like I had a limb cut off. Every morning I wait for her to get up and start getting ready for school and when she doesn't I go to her room and open the door and all I see is this perfect room, the bed made, no dirty clothes on the floor, her desk uncluttered, her stuffed animals in a tidy circle on her bed the way she liked to put them." He paused. "So I look at her pictures on my computer and play home movies, and she stays alive for me that way. It helps me get through the day."

Lori-Anne reached for his arm. "That's why I want you to try some medication."

"But don't you get it?" He pulled his arm away. "I don't want to stop feeling bad because if I do, I might stop thinking of her and remembering her."

Lori-Anne shook her head. "Torturing yourself isn't healthy, it doesn't prove how much you loved her. Staying in a state of pain isn't the way to remember her. She was our daughter and she was beautiful and wonderful and we need to remember her that way. You will not forget her if you're happy. If you're happy you'll be able to appreciate the joy she brought us. If you're happy, we'll be able to move forward with her in our hearts."

"What if you're wrong?"

"I'm not."

"You can't know that."

"Do some research. Talk to your doctor. Connect with people who've gone through something similar. We can join a bereavement group. I'm sure there's something out there to help us. I'm willing to try anything. Matt, please. Don't you want to feel better?"

He couldn't look her in the eye.

⋆ ⋆

Lori-Anne had been talking with her mother for over an hour, the two of them sitting at the kitchen table, a couple of empty Tim Horton's coffee cups in front of them. She'd been venting and her mother had been listening, never choosing sides but offering advice when appropriate. Victoria had always liked Mathieu so Lori-Anne wasn't surprised that her mother didn't say anything bad about him. She'd say *he's hurting* or *he'd always wanted a big family so this is hard for him* or *he's proud and doesn't want to appear weak, that's why he won't go on medication.*

Well-intended words, but they didn't change the situation. She and Mathieu were in a horrible place and it wasn't going to change soon.

"I just wish none of this had happened," Lori-Anne said. "Maybe if I'd taken the Pathfinder . . ."

"Why didn't you?"

"Mathieu had needed it earlier to go down to WoodSource and get some supplies, and since I'd been using his car that day, I just didn't think to switch."

"We don't know that it would have made a difference."

"It's bigger and has airbags."

"Now you're torturing yourself, honey."

Lori-Anne tore up the napkin she held in her hand. "I'm losing my husband."

"He'll come around."

"And if he doesn't?"

"You'll be fine," her father said from the living room.

"You have something to say, Dad?"

Samuel Weatherly came and stood at the edge of the kitchen. "Mathieu has never been the right man for you. I think you could have done better."

"Dad!"

Samuel shrugged.

"You can't just say that and not explain yourself."

He looked at her. "You were so driven all your life until you met him, and then you changed. It was like he held you back."

"I disagree," she said. "When I met him I was lost and broken-hearted from my affair and Mathieu gave me what I needed. He's exactly the sort of man I need. Kind, attentive, and passionate. With him, I was able to slow my life down and enjoy it instead of chasing an ideal that you planted in me when I was just a child. You don't like him because you lost control over me, isn't that right?"

"Oh Lori-Anne," Victoria said. "Your father didn't mean that."

Lori-Anne turned to her mother. "Please Mom, let him defend himself. You've always tried to explain Dad's actions to us kids, and I for one stopped believing in your explanations long ago." She returned her attention to her father. "I love Mathieu, and even though we're going through a tough time right now—how could we not after losing our only daughter . . ." She paused and waited to regain her composure. "I'm not leaving him. He's the one who will have to end our marriage if that's what he wants. So please, stop hating him."

"I don't hate him," Samuel said, taking a seat at the kitchen table. "I just think you could have been much more."

"Dad, I'm a marketing director. I earn a darn good salary. I've taken care of my family. So what if I'm not running your company. I didn't want it."

"But you could be," he said.

"I don't want to," she said. "And Jim, the idiot that he is, would be devastated."

"He'd get over it," Samuel said. "I've always thought you had the better business acumen."

"Sorry to disappoint you again, but no thanks. I love my job and I love my husband. That's my life. That's what I want back. I just pray it's what Mathieu wants."

"Why wouldn't he?" her mother said.

Lori-Anne chewed her lower lip, a habit she'd had since she was four years old. Her father would scold her for something, and she'd stand there looking up at him, biting her lip and trying hard not to cry.

"I think he blames me," she said.

"It was an accident, honey," her mother said while reaching for Lori-Anne's hand. "It was an accident."

Lori-Anne pulled her hand away and snatched another napkin from the napkin holder. She folded it in half, then again, and again until it was as small as it would fold.

"I wanted Nadia to tell me what was wrong, why the moods lately? Something was going on and I wanted her to know that I was there for her. But she wouldn't tell me. Kept saying I was imagining things, that nothing was wrong."

Lori-Anne started to unfold the napkin.

"She was texting on her phone and I asked her to stop so we could talk, but she didn't. I got angry and reached for her phone, and the light turned yellow . . ."

Lori-Anne tore the napkin in half, then again, and again until it lay in a pile with the other torn napkin. She hadn't told her family exactly what had happened. She'd only said that the roads had been slippery from the snow and that she hadn't been able to stop in time. She'd said that the car making the left-hand turn should have seen that she couldn't stop and should have waited until she'd cleared the intersection.

But that was only partially true.

If she hadn't been so dead set on getting Nadia's phone, she would have seen that she did have time to stop, even on the slippery road. But because she didn't stop, the truck behind her followed her through the intersection and their car got wedged between the Lexus SUV and the black Ford F150. Mathieu's eleven-year-old Honda Civic didn't have airbags and the F150 crushed the passenger side like an accordion. Lori-Anne couldn't believe that she'd had only cuts and bruises while Nadia had been killed instantly.

"So you see," she said after telling her parents almost everything—there was one last bit she'd kept to herself because it was too painful to share, "it's my fault. I was careless and my daughter is dead because of it. And my husband hates me right now. He won't say the words, but I feel it, the anger in his voice, the way he looks at me, the way he won't touch me."

"Honey," Victoria said. "I wish you'd told us sooner. We could have helped you get through this."

"I don't know what to do," Lori-Anne said. "I'm afraid to tell him what really happened. I just don't see what good that'll do. Except that I'm carrying it like a burden and I think he senses my guilt. If I tell him, I could lose him."

"You have to tell him," Victoria said. "Honesty is always best. A solid marriage is built on honesty."

Lori-Anne could see her mother pinning her father with her eyes and sensed there was some double meaning in those words. Someday she would have to have a long talk with her mother about her father. There was something there—Lori-Anne had felt it for a very long time.

"What if it kills the last bit of life our marriage has?"

"He's a good man who's hurting right now," Victoria said. "He's angry, but not at you. He's angry at the situation. He's lost. I know that he loves you."

Lori-Anne shook her head. "I'm not so sure, Mom. We don't even share the same bed these days."

"Oh honey! You have to tell him."

"Aren't you listening to what she's saying?" Samuel said.

"Of course I am," Victoria said. "After all, I'm the one who saved our marriage."

Samuel opened his mouth and closed it again. He stood and left the kitchen.

"Mom?"

Victoria shook her head. "Not today."

"But—"

"Never mind that old coot," she said. "You need to save your marriage, and it might not be easy, but if you truly love Mathieu, you'll persevere, you will support him, you will give him love. Most of all, you will give him your heart."

"Oh Mom," Lori-Anne said. "What if he breaks it?"

"Then he breaks it," Victoria said. "But at least you'll know you gave it your all."

CB ᑭꝝ

Mathieu knocked and stepped inside his grandparents' home. He hugged and kissed his grandmother on the cheek. "Happy Mother's Day."

"Thank you, dear," she said, the words slurring off her tongue. "How did you get here?"

"Took a cab," he said. "Guess I should think of getting a new car."

"Maybe you should get yourself a truck," Grandpa said from the comfort of the couch in the living room. "Would be handy."

"I did think of that," Mathieu said and followed his grand-mother into the room. "It would make it easier when I get supplies."

Grandpa folded the paper he'd been reading and put it on the glass-top coffee table, one of Mathieu's early woodworking projects when he was fifteen. "So, how's that wife of yours?"

"She's fine," Mathieu said. He looked down at his bandaged finger. "I guess."

"Oh sweetheart," Grandma said. "What's wrong?"

Mathieu shrugged. The last thing he wanted was to burden them with his problems. Especially Grandma. She'd lost a lot of strength since the stroke.

"We're not really getting along," he said, feeling ashamed. "She wants me to go on meds."

"It could help," Grandma said. "It's worth trying, don't you think?"

"No marriage is perfect," Grandpa said, looking at his wife. "Sharing your life with someone can be trying at times. But it's that sharing that builds a bond between two people and makes it nearly unbreakable. Sounds like Lori-Anne is looking after that bond. Are you?"

"I just can't let go of Nadia," he said, remembering how tiny she once was and how she fit perfectly in his arms. "I want to hold her so badly."

"What's that got to do with medication?" Grandpa said. "You think medication will make you forget your daughter?"

"You don't understand," Mathieu said.

Grandpa didn't get angry often, but his eyes hardened. "I think we know exactly what you're going through, young man. When your parents died in the car crash, you think that was easy on us? When your Aunt Jacqueline passed away of cancer the day of 9/11, you think that was easy on us?"

"I'm sorry," Mathieu said. "I didn't mean . . . it's just so hard."

"When your father died," Grandma said, "I had awful nightmares."

Mathieu sat a little straighter, his eyes widening. "I thought I was the one who had nightmares."

"We both did," Grandma said. "And looking after you was my way of coming to terms with the death of your father. When I held you, I held him. I remembered him as a boy. I thanked the Lord every day that you'd survived that crash. You were my medication."

"I . . . I never thought of it that way," Mathieu said.

"It was hard on your grandmother," Grandpa said. "I'd often find her sitting at the kitchen table, leafing through old photo albums. Back then we didn't know what she was going through, but today she'd be diagnosed with depression."

Mathieu shook his head. "I'm not depressed. I miss my daughter, that's all."

"How do you sleep?" Grandpa said.

"Not great."

"How's work? You mentioned you've fallen behind," Grandpa said.

"I'll catch up."

"You just said things with Lori-Anne aren't going well. Sounds like you should be doing everything you can to help yourself get better. Are you?"

Mathieu looked down at his finger again.

"There's no shame in admitting you're going through a depression," Grandpa said. "It's a lot easier to get help these days. Have you seen your doctor?"

"No."

"You really should," Grandma said. "Those two years after your father died were pretty bad. If it wasn't for your grandfather . . ."

"Two years?" Mathieu said.

"I was in a bad place. I'd see something on TV and start crying because it reminded me of your father. I'd be making your favourite meal, folding your laundry, vacuuming your room, and all these things reminded me of when your father was your age and I'd start to cry."

"I never noticed," Mathieu said. "I mean, I never saw you cry. You always had a smile on your face. You always comforted me when I woke up screaming at night."

"Your needs came first, honey. You were hurting too, and you were so young and you needed me. I grieved when you weren't around."

"I have no one who needs me that much," Mathieu said. "Maybe if we had another child, I'd be able to do like you did."

"That's where you're wrong," Grandpa said. "You have a wife who needs you."

Mathieu shook his head. "She's got her work. That's her escape."

"Maybe it's because she can't count on you," Grandpa said.

"Your grandfather is right, honey."

Mathieu plucked woodchips off his pants. Maybe he should have changed his clothes before coming here, but the argument with Lori-Anne had left him rattled.

"Go see a doctor," Grandma said. "Don't lose Lori-Anne because you're stubborn."

"I'm not being stubborn," he said, a little too harshly. "Sorry, Grandma. I'm just . . . I'm just tired."

"You need a good night's sleep," Grandpa said. "And you need to lighten your load. Listen to your wife."

Mathieu sat back and rubbed his face with both hands. Everyone was telling him the same thing that he didn't want to hear. He missed his daughter and he didn't see how being on medication could help. What he needed was to be left alone so he could grieve.

Two years.

That's what his grandmother had said. It had taken her two years to get over the death of his father. Nadia had been gone seven weeks. He had another twenty-two months. That seemed way too long. He felt sure that in a few weeks things would turn around, he'd start to feel better. Maybe if he didn't, then he'd think about seeing his doctor.

He stood and stared at the painting on the opposite wall. The painting had been there forever, but he felt that he was seeing it for the first time. The artist had captured the very essence of a new beginning: a beautiful sunrise over the ocean horizon.

Grandpa followed Mathieu's gaze. "I bought that in 1949 just after we got married. Seemed like it was calling me. Never been to wherever that is, but it reminds me that each day brings new possibilities."

What Mathieu saw was an explosion of colours far away in the distance, almost a mirage really, forever out of reach.

SEVEN

Victoria Day
May 21, 2012
9:43 a.m.

Mathieu had put it off as long as he could, but today he needed to get going on that little girl's bed if he was going to deliver it in eight weeks. He grabbed a cup of coffee and headed for the garage to go over the plan and materials. He was measuring a slab of cherry when he heard the sound of a coasting bicycle approaching fast. He turned just in time to see Caitlin dismount her bike and drop it on the driveway.

"This is a pleasant surprise," he said, putting his measuring tape down on the workbench and placing a pencil behind his ear. "What brings you here?"

"I didn't feel like hanging around our house," Caitlin said and walked into the garage. "I hope you don't mind me dropping by like this?"

"Any time," he said. "You're always welcome here. Anything going on at home?"

"Not really. Nick is sleeping, mom is doing laundry, and Suzie spent the night at her boyfriend's like she does every week-end. It was just boring."

"Well not much excitement here either."

Caitlin looked at the pieces of wood scattered about. "What're you making?"

"A bed for a little girl."

"Like Nadia's?"

"Pretty much."

"That little girl is going to love it. Nadia was so lucky you made nice furniture for her."

"I don't think she always felt that way."

"Probably not," Caitlin said and ran her fingers along a smooth piece of mahogany. "Kids don't appreciate stuff like that. I should know, I'm one. We always think if it doesn't come from a store it's no good."

"You might be right."

They stood silent for a moment but it was broken by the neighbour's irrigation system rising out of the ground like camouflaged soldiers, a half-dozen sprinkler heads on the attack. A lawnmower roared to life in the distance.

"I miss her," Caitlin said. She wrapped her arms around herself and crunched her face. "I want my cousin back. I really do. It's not fair."

Mathieu pulled her into him and felt her shake.

"I wish we could get her back too," he said. "But we can't."

"My heart aches so much," she said. "I sometimes want to pull it out to stop the pain."

"I know how that feels," Mathieu said, barely above a whisper. "Missing someone is just about the hardest pain in the world, especially when we know that person can't come back. We hurt because she meant so much to us. You don't hurt for someone you didn't love, and we sure loved her."

Caitlin stepped away from Mathieu and wiped her tears with the back of her hand. "I miss her more than I miss my dad."

"I guess things are pretty crappie at home."

"Yeah," Caitlin said and stared at her feet. "Dad moved in with some other woman. I think she works for him. He was coming to get the rest of his things today so that's really why I didn't want to be home. I'm pissed at him."

"I can understand."

"It's not fair. He's messing up everything. He doesn't care about us. As long as he's happy, right? But what about me? I hate him right now for what he's doing. Is that wrong?"

Mathieu shrugged. "Does it feel wrong?"

She shook her head. "I don't know. Maybe a little. I don't wish him dead or anything, but I don't really want to see him either. I just get so mad when I see him. So many of my friends have divorced parents but I never thought it would happen to my parents. I always thought they loved each other."

"Sometimes, people change. Life can do that."

Caitlin looked up at her uncle. "Are things better with you and Aunt Lori-Anne?"

How did Caitlin know? Was the family talking, or did she just pick up on it? Kids, especially teenagers, noticed things. How could he explain to his fourteen-year-old niece the loneliness of a shattered marriage? It wasn't enough to still love Lori-Anne. Something was missing, and every day the emptiness in their house reminded him of that.

"I honestly don't know," he said after a moment. "We're having some difficulties right now but I'm sure it'll get better."

"I hope you don't get a divorce too," Caitlin said. "It's bad enough my parents are. I don't think Nadia would want you guys to. That would so double suck."

"Things sure seem to suck lately, that's for sure." He took the pencil from behind his ear and started to drum it against the thumb of his left hand. "We're all going through some tough times right now."

"My mom drinks too much."

"I know. I'm sorry."

"I tried it a while back, to see why she did it," Caitlin said, a grimace on her face. "It burned my throat like bad medicine. I know kids in my class who get drunk all the time and they talk about it like it's so great. But I bet they never see their mom drunk and throwing up and falling to pieces."

"I'm sure they don't," he said. "I know things look shitty for you, but it will get better."

"I guess if Nadia was still here, maybe my parents getting a divorce wouldn't bum me out so much. But without her . . . it's like . . . you know. I would feel so much better if I still had her."

"Yeah," Mathieu said and swallowed a bag of nails. "We all would."

EIGHT

June 14, 2012
5:59 p.m.

L ori-Anne stood in front of the Father's Day card display at the Hallmark store, unable to find something that was appropriate. The covers were wrong, the wording was wrong, the entire idea was wrong. What had possessed her to stop in the first place? After the Mother's Day fiasco, why bother?

They weren't parents to anyone anymore.

"Damn it." She put the card back and hurried out of the store. She slammed the car door, threw her purse on the passenger seat, and drove away. Maybe ignoring Father's Day was the best thing to do. She'd just thought that if she did something nice, something from the heart, that maybe it would pull Mathieu out of that shell he'd been hiding in for the last two months. She was so tired of being alone and just wanted to feel the tenderness of his fingers against her flesh, the security of his arms around her as they lay in bed, the affirmation that they were still a couple.

She longed for the way he once looked at her, not goofy or anything, but with so much want in his eyes that she found herself light-headed from the joy that burst inside her. He made her feel alive and desired and his, which wasn't a bad thing. It was an incredible high to be loved that much by another person. His passion quenched the thirst she'd been missing in relationships with other men. After her failed affair with her English professor, Lori-Anne had found her prince charming in this young, idealistic Mathieu. It had not taken long for her to realize that he was exactly the gentle sort of man that she'd been looking for and needed.

That Mathieu had to be there behind that wall of depression. She really believed that. Once in a while, she saw glimpses of him, but his grief kept pulling him away. The more she tried to help, the further adrift they seemed to be.

Lori-Anne pulled in behind the Buick and killed the engine before she realized that she'd driven to Mathieu's grandparents' place. Since she was here, she got out and rang the bell.

"It's so nice to see you," Grandpa said as he let her in. "You're alone?"

"Yes," she said. "I was heading home but somehow ended up here. Hope you don't mind, but maybe we can talk?"

"Join us in the kitchen," he said. "I'm making dinner. Did you want to eat with us?"

"I don't want to intrude—"

"Nonsense," he said. "Got plenty. I won't take no for an answer."

Lori-Anne had always loved this about Grandpa—she pretty much had come to think of both of them as her own grandparents especially since hers had been deceased for quite some time—the way they made her feel welcomed all the time. He and Grandma had always been great listeners, and maybe she needed that right now.

"Thank you," she said and sat at the small round kitchen table. "How are you doing, Grandma?"

"I'm fine, dear," she said. Her speech had a permanent slur now. "A little frustrating not being able to do as much as I used to."

"She saw her doctor yesterday," Grandpa said. "He told her to take it one day at a time. She could live fine for another ten years without another episode—"

"Or I could have another stroke tomorrow," Grandma finished.

"Oh, I hope not," Lori-Anne said. "Just take it easy. You deserve it."

"I've lived a good, long life. A happy one. Sure we had struggles, but Leon made it all worth it. He's been a good man."

Leon kissed his wife on the forehead.

Feeling a little uncomfortable, Lori-Anne looked away, thinking that's what she wanted with Mathieu. When she's eighty-plus years old she still wants him to look at her the way he did when she was twenty-three. Grandpa and Grandma were proof that love could last forever.

"No more talk like that," Grandpa said. "We're depressing Lori-Anne."

"Just seeing how much the two of you still love each other, that leaves a girl's heart full of hope," Lori-Anne said. "Speaking of depression, has Mathieu said anything to you two?"

"We haven't seen him since Mother's Day," Grandpa said. "Called him a couple of times but he cut it short, saying he was busy trying to catch up on orders."

"He did fall behind," Lori-Anne said. "I'd hoped that he'd at least spoken with you guys."

"Things aren't good lately, are they?" Grandpa said.

Lori-Anne shook her head. "I'd like to lie and say they are, but they're not. We barely talk. I just don't know what to do."

"You keep trying," Grandpa said. He finished putting the garden salad together and put the bowl on the table. He put three handfuls of noodles into a boiling pot of water and stirred the simmering spaghetti sauce. Garlic bread in the oven smelled like warm buttery comfort.

"That smells so good," Lori-Anne said. Her stomach growled, reminding her that she'd skipped lunch again. "He always treats you this good?" she said to Grandma.

Grandma smiled. "You know, we've always leaned on each other. I had an awful time when Denis passed away. We tried to tell Mathieu this, how we ended up seeing a counsellor to help me cope, but he wasn't interested. Medication is so much better than back then."

Grandpa put three plates on the table. "He can be a bit stubborn."

"Denis sure was," Grandma said and took a mouthful of her dinner. "This is wonderful, dear."

"Well, it's your recipe so it ought to be," Grandpa said. "Dig in Lori-Anne."

They ate in silence for a few minutes, the cutlery clinking against dinnerware. Grandpa brought out a bottle of red wine and Lori-Anne couldn't pass that up. She couldn't remember the last time she'd enjoyed an actual dinner.

"How did you do it?" Lori-Anne asked once she finished eating. "Get through it, I mean."

"We talked," Grandpa said. "And we listened. I guess what we had was trust in each other. Not many marriages last without trust."

"How can I get Mathieu to trust me?"

"You need to talk, the two of you," Grandpa said.

"He doesn't want to. And I'm slowly giving up."

"You can't," Grandpa said as he pushed his empty plate to the side and tackled his salad. "He's angry. Flore wasn't angry, she was just sad. Mathieu's anger is a barrier that you'll need to get through. It's not going to be easy, I'm afraid. We'll keep trying too."

"Thank you, but it almost sounds hopeless," Lori-Anne said. "He has to want to work it out, but without a clear mind, I don't see that happening."

"Problem is that right now Mathieu can't see the end of his grief. He's an emotional boy. I remember when he tore the ligaments in his knee and his hockey dreams ended. He was miserable for months."

Grandma nodded. "Oh my, was he ever. Didn't matter what we said to him. He'd had his sights on a hockey career for years.

Dreamed of playing in the NHL and he was really good so maybe it would have happened."

"But this is much more than that," Lori-Anne said. "His knee healed and he moved on. Nadia is gone for good. How can he heal from that?"

"Stick with him and he'll come through," Grandpa said.

"I want to believe you so badly," she said. "I want my husband back, but—"

"It's hard," Grandpa said.

"Like you can't imagine," she said.

"Don't give up," Grandma said. "He's lucky to have you and he'll come around. Have faith."

"I think I need more than that. I need a miracle."

Grandma reached across the table for her hand. "We've always loved you, and we're sure that Mathieu does too. He needs you to stay strong. Your strength will get you both through this. We believe in you."

Lori-Anne smiled. It was nice to hear how others saw her, but there were times when she looked at herself in the mirror and didn't see a strong or confident woman. She saw a little girl who was in way over her head.

And knowing that it was up to her to save her marriage left her feeling like bees were ripping apart her insides, desperately trying to get out.

NINE

M athieu pushed Nadia's bedroom door open and stood in the doorway. Her room looked the same as the day before, and the day before that. It hadn't changed in nearly three months, frozen in time, a reminder that a life had come to an abrupt halt. He stared at a poster of Kurt Cobain. Just a few months ago it had been all about Justin Bieber. It had been Justin this and Justin that. Mathieu would cringe when she mentioned his name.

And almost overnight, Nirvana's front man had appeared. And then her rollercoaster moods had started.

He picked up her iPod and skimmed through the play list: Nirvana, Green Day, Blink 182, Interpol, She Wants Revenge. His little girl had changed, pulling a one eighty. What had happened? Maybe Lori-Anne had been on to something when she'd mentioned that maybe Nadia had been trying drugs. Except the day of her funeral hadn't been the day to bring that up.

Now he wondered.

It would explain the turnaround. Hadn't he smelled smoke on Nadia and Caitlin? Yes, Nancy smoked and it could be residue on Caitlin, but on Nadia? He knew kids her age tried pot, but he'd always hoped that she'd be above that. Parents didn't want their kids to get hurt, parents didn't want their kids to do anything wrong, parents didn't want their kids to grow up. But the days of being Nadia's hero were in the rear-view mirror of his life.

Mathieu remembered how she'd kept dropping her iPod, so he'd gone out one day after New Year's to buy one of those gel covers. It had saved the iPod on several occasions. He put it back on the night table and moved toward her bookshelf: The Harry Potter books, the Twilight series, the Hunger Games trilogy. Nadia had loved to read. That too had stopped just a few months ago.

Why?

He pulled her grade six yearbook from the shelf and leafed through it, seeing a couple of pictures of Nadia and Caitlin. They looked so much younger just two years ago. Kids. Good kids. Still innocent.

No smoking.

No attitude.

He put the yearbook back and sat at her desk. He powered up Nadia's laptop. A birthday present, this past February. She'd begged for that more than the iPod. He and Lori-Anne figured she could use it for homework assignments. Mostly though, she used it for Facebook. All the kids used Facebook. It was the way they socialized. Strange how social media was such a big thing, yet to Mathieu, it seemed to lack the main aspect of socializing: people getting together. Sure, the kids had hundreds of friends, virtual friends, but really, who was kidding who? How many of those so-called friends actually knew you? A dozen? Half a dozen? One or two?

His fingers hovered over the keyboard, barely touching the keys. He was being critical. It wasn't his generation. He didn't quite understand them. It was a parent thing. Each generation never quite got the other.

Then again, he loved to use the internet for research. He'd discovered all sorts of nice woodworking projects online. He'd even joined a chat group of woodworkers and exchanged ideas regularly with people he'd never met in person.

The world was simply different.

Smaller but a little lonelier.

"What are you doing?" Lori-Anne said.

Mathieu turned and saw his wife standing in the doorway. She never entered Nadia's room. The last time he'd pointed that out, it had turned into a vicious fight. He had accused her of not caring, of not loving their dead daughter. Lori-Anne had said nothing. She had not cried. She had iced him with her eyes, and walked away.

Nadia had been gone only a week.

He had run after her, shouting from the top of the stairs about how cold she was and what was she scared of, it was just a room. Lori-Anne paused halfway down the staircase, but held her tongue. Still, nothing had been the same since.

"I'm just sitting here, taking in who she was. It brings me closer to her. Sometimes I can even smell her, the way she smelled after her bath when she was a baby. The Ivory soap on her skin, the baby shampoo. It's all here," he said with a hand gesture. "If you came in, you'd feel it too."

Lori-Anne stared him down.

"I didn't mean that," he said quietly. "I just meant—"

"I know what you meant," she said. "Just let it be."

"Yeah, sure," he said. "Sorry."

They looked at each other for a second or two, and then Mathieu turned back to the laptop to get away from her gaze.

"We should talk," Lori-Anne said, crossing her arms.

"We're talking now."

She pressed her lips into a thin line. "I mean about what's going on between us."

"Okay," he said.

"Can you look at me?"

Mathieu did but struggled not to turn away. The way Lori-Anne pinned him with her stare, cold and angry, but also vulnerable, afraid to get hurt put him on edge. He really didn't want to have a fight. Not this morning. He just wanted to remember his daughter and pretend that she was still with them. He wanted to be a father on Father's Day.

Was that too much to ask?

"Look, I'll call my parents and tell them I'm not coming over so we can work a few things out."

"But it's Father's Day. Don't you want to see your dad?"

"I've been a little mad at him lately."

Mathieu didn't say anything. He felt the same way about his father-in-law. Polite acknowledgment of one another best described their relationship. If it could be called that. The old man had never approved of Mathieu although Mathieu had never done anything to cause Samuel to have this animosity toward him. He'd stopped looking for his approval long ago.

He was simply Lori-Anne's father.

"So, can we talk about us?" Lori-Anne said.

"We used to ride our bikes a lot back then," he said, looking at the 8x10 picture hanging on the wall, showing the three of them on their bikes. Nadia had been three or four and sat in the bike seat behind Mathieu. He'd put the camera on the hood of the car and set the timer while Lori-Anne held his bike until he mounted it. Not the best picture but Nadia had liked it.

"We went to Rockcliffe that day."

Lori-Anne leaned against the doorframe. The hardness in her eyes faded. "Yeah. We rode around and looked at all those expensive homes."

"We stopped at a park because Nadia was having a bird. She had to play there. It had this thing you hang on to and it slides across a long steel beam. What do you call that?"

She shrugged.

"We had fun," he said, still looking at the picture. "We used to have simple fun outings. Nadia fell asleep in her seat on the way back to the car. Her head kept swinging from side to side and I had a hard time balancing the bike."

Lori-Anne smiled. "I'd forgotten about that. I was laughing so hard and you were all uptight about losing your balance."

He looked at her, pensive. "Where did all those fun days go?"

"I don't know," she said, planting her right foot against the doorframe. "I really don't know."

A silence fell between them. Mathieu's gaze returned to the picture on the wall. A small sensation ignited inside his chest, a flicker of happiness that burned out too quickly.

"Life was good then," he said. "We were good."

"It can be again," Lori-Anne said. "We can be."

He turned to her. "Do you really believe that?"

"Yes," she said. "It will never be the same. We're changed forever by what happened. But why can't we find some sort of happiness together again?"

He rubbed the two-day growth on his chin.

"Want to give it a try?" she said. "Give us a chance?"

"I just need . . ." he said.

"What?" she said, looking at him. "What do you need? Tell me what I can do to help you. Don't shut me out anymore. We need each other to get through this."

He shook his head. "I don't know."

"Maybe we should see a counsellor."

"Like a shrink?"

"Someone with experience and knowledge who can help us, yes."

He shifted on the chair. "I'd rather not."

"Mathieu," she said, "We need help. I see it, why can't you?"

He scratched the back of his neck. "I just need a bit of time."

"It's been three months!"

"SO!" he said, an explosion of anger darkening his eyes. "If I need a year, so be it. Just because you've moved on doesn't mean that I'm ready. Damn it, I miss her so much."

"And I miss her too," she said. "I love Nadia as much as you do. Maybe I wasn't with her as much, but you can't fault me for that, and you can't think that I loved her or miss her any less. She was my daughter too."

"So how can you forget her so easily?"

"Who says I forgot her?" she said with a defensive hand gesture. "I can't believe you said that."

"It's what I see," he said. "You went back to work just a few days after we buried her. What am I supposed to think?"

"You know what?" she said. "I don't give a damn what you think. I can't believe this. It's absolutely insane. Are you listening to yourself? Just because I drag myself to work every day and pour my energy into something else for a while doesn't mean I'm not in pain. My work is my therapy. It's a routine that's helping me get on with life without my daughter in it."

She turned her head to hide her coming tears.

"Sorry," he said. He took a step toward her but she stepped back. "You just don't seem to be in as much pain as me—"

"Who says I'm not?"

"I . . . I . . ."

"You know," she said, "I was hoping we could spend the day together and figure things out and get us back on track. But I don't think you want the same thing. I don't know what you want. Do you? Huh? Because if you do, then I sure hope you'll

tell me someday so we can save what we have left. Just don't
wait too long or we'll have nothing left to save."

Before he could say anything, Lori-Anne strode down the
hallway to their room and slammed the door. He took a few
steps, then stopped.

He put his fist through the wall, the plasterboard crumbling
to the floor.

"Fuck!" Holding his throbbing hand, Mathieu hurried down
the stairs and slammed the front door on his way out, not both-
ering to lock it. He got in the Pathfinder, the tires squealing as
he gunned the engine. He drove too fast through the neighbourhood, blaring the horn and jamming on the brakes when
someone backed out of their driveway without looking. Mathieu
swerved and gave the guy the finger. At the intersection, stopped
by a red light, he slapped the steering wheel with his aching
hand. Pain shot to his elbow. "Damnit!" Someone gave him a
polite honk and Mathieu flipped him the bird. He needed to get
away, get somewhere that wasn't so bloody busy. He made a left
on Jock Street and followed it to the end, by then knowing
where he was headed. He hadn't been there since the funeral,
not because he hadn't wanted to, but because he'd been unable
to find his courage.

Today, he needed to go.

Mathieu parked the car at the edge of the cemetery and
watched as people came and went in their cars. Groups of
mourners walked the grounds, small families huddled together,
an older woman stood alone in front of a tombstone. After a
few minutes he turned the radio station to the one Nadia liked,

and listened to the music she'd listened to lately. He heard a lot of songs he'd once liked too, but over the years he'd pretty much listened to whatever Lori-Anne or Nadia wanted to listen to. As long as they were happy, he was fine with that. That's really all he'd ever wanted, for the two women in his life to be happy.

His conversation with Lori-Anne played in his mind. All she wanted was for the two of them to be happy again, to make a life again, to find love again. He got all of that. It's just that he wasn't there yet, and didn't know if and when he'd get there. For him, it was simply too soon.

He looked toward Nadia's grave. It felt surreal that his daughter, that beautiful little girl who had once fit in the palm of his hand, was nothing but ashes. That reality tightened the muscles in his stomach, and his jaw clenched so hard it ached. How did someone find happiness after such a loss? Was it possible?

After an hour he pulled away and merged with the traffic, his mind unable to convince his legs to step out of the car and make the walk to her gravesite. He'd come here tormented and consumed by rage, weighted down by feelings of worthlessness, and now he was leaving with his heart filled with shameful regrets. He saw a semi-transport coming in the opposite lane and slowly drifted toward it. To end this misery, to finally get relief, could be that simple. But then he pulled the car back and brought it to a stop on the shoulder, a shiver running up his spine even though the temperature gauge on the dashboard indicated that it was already twenty-six degrees Celsius outside.

A gorgeous early summer's day.

Except that Mathieu couldn't shake that shiver. He would never tell anyone, but he was certain that Nadia had just saved his life, her hands on top of his hands, steering the car away from the approaching death that he'd been so sure was the answer to the torture his life had become.

TEN

Canada Day
July 1, 2012
9:39 a.m.

C anada's birthday arrived hot and humid, no clouds,
and plenty of festivities. Being the capital of the coun-
try, Ottawa always put on a great fireworks event
downtown, and several of the surrounding communities also ca-
tered to their constituents, especially to the young kids. Over the
last few years, Bridgehaven had been putting on a full day of
activities with rides, games, and music, and Nadia had loved going. Last year she'd brought a couple of friends in addition to
Caitlin, who had joined them with Nancy and Nicholas.

Lori-Anne and Mathieu would be skipping those activities
this year. Since Father's Day, they'd grown further apart. Lori-
Anne did her thing and Mathieu did his, the two never meeting
in the middle, no meals shared on top of not sharing a bed. It
seemed their relationship was heading one way, and it wasn't the
right way. They'd become strangers living under the same roof.

Lori-Anne watched Mathieu from the living-room window.
He was washing his new truck. Last week he'd gone out and

come home with it, taking whatever was on the lot. The new models were coming in so all the dealerships had great deals on. Lori-Anne thought if she and Nadia had been in that big new F150 instead of the old Civic, well things wouldn't be where they were.

She finished her coffee and put the empty cup on the little table in the foyer and went outside. She was still in her pajamas. At the end of the walkway she stopped, not wanting to get sprayed.

"Hey," she said.

Mathieu gave a nod her way. "Hey."

Even though it was already hot, she wrapped her arms around herself like she was cold. She felt something drop into the abyss of her stomach, her heart probably. This is what they'd become, two people who didn't even know what to say to one another, unless they were tearing each other apart.

"Do you have plans for today?" she said.

Mathieu rinsed the rear left tire. "Not really. Probably just work on that little girl's bed. I'm almost done and then I need to apply the finish so they can pick it up at the end of the month."

Lori-Anne looked away, her heart sinking deeper. "Guess you don't want to go downtown later?"

"Not really."

"Seems like you just don't want me around."

He rinsed the side of his truck. "Not sure what you expect from me. You've moved on and I can't. Not sure where that leaves us?"

"Pretty much where we are."

Mathieu turned to her. "And that's my fault?"

"I didn't say that."

"You didn't need to."

Lori-Anne took a breath and waited for the venom she felt rising inside of her to retreat. When she didn't say anything Mathieu turned his back and continued washing the truck. It would be so easy to follow this where it was headed, to let her frustration and hurt erupt from her with harsh and stabbing words, but she knew it wouldn't make her feel better. It never did.

Lori-Anne went back in the house feeling like her marriage was over and it was only a matter of time before one of them asked for a divorce. She was starting to believe that it might be the right thing to do. She didn't want to admit failure, but it was getting impossible to deny. This life was sucking all her energy and maybe getting away from Mathieu, at least for a while, would do them both good. If only she could trust that he wouldn't do something drastic.

She wouldn't be able live with the guilt of walking away if he did. But she couldn't stay with him the way he was, either.

An hour later she left for her parents'. She needed to talk to her mom.

C3 80

"I don't know what to do with Mathieu," Lori-Anne said, barging in as soon as her mother opened the front door. "He won't talk to me. I try but it's like he doesn't care. He's just—"

Victoria gestured with her eyes toward the kitchen. Lori-Anne peeked and saw her niece sitting at the kitchen table, eating a croissant.

"Oh sweetie," Lori-Anne said. "How did you get here?"

"I rode my bike. Only took thirty minutes."

"Is that all?" Lori-Anne said. "Yeah, I guess it's not that far from home. Sorry you had to hear what I said."

"I know how Uncle Mathieu feels," Caitlin said and pushed her empty plate. "I can spend hours in my room lying on my bed, just missing Nadia. Sometimes I grab my phone to text her and then realize I won't get an answer, and I just cry. It really sucks, you know."

"I know," Lori-Anne said and took a seat at the kitchen table. She reached for a croissant piled on a plate in the middle of the table. "But we all need to move forward, somehow. I know it sounds cold, but what else can we do?"

Victoria joined them. "It's not cold, honey. It's reality. It doesn't make it any less painful but we all need, as a family, to support each other and move on."

Lori-Anne picked at her croissant and put small pieces in her mouth. Her appetite wasn't there so she put the rest of the croissant on a napkin. "I don't know how to help him do that. I sound like a broken record, but how do I get Mathieu the help he needs when he doesn't want it? Sometimes I just wish he'd say it so we can get on with it."

"Say what?" Caitlin said.

"That he blames me for the accident. After all, I was driving."

"It was an accident, Aunt Lori-Anne."

"I know, sweetie, but if he needs to blame someone to be able to move forward, then so be it. We can't stay how we are."

"You won't get a divorce, too?"

Lori-Anne rubbed her forehead. "I might be angry with your uncle but I'm not getting a divorce. Adults fight too. We just need to work things out. Somehow."

"How come my parents couldn't do that?"

Lori-Anne shook her head. "I can't answer that. A couple needs a lot of love to get through the crap that happens."

"Guess my dad stopped loving my mom," Caitlin said, as if talking to herself. "Or he loved that other woman more. I hate her. And him."

"I know it's tough on you." Lori-Anne moved closer and put an arm around her niece's shoulder. "Life doesn't always play fair, sweetie. We'll get through it."

"You can't promise that," Caitlin said. "You can't know that. It could keep getting worse and worse."

"I sure hope not."

"But it could," Caitlin said. "When you came in, you sounded so mad at Uncle Mathieu, like you hated him."

Lori-Anne pulled her arm away and let her shoulders drop. "I wouldn't say I hate him. I'm just really disappointed and frustrated. He's impossible to be around with these days and I don't know what to do about it. He won't listen to anything I say. He won't get help. I'm mad at him because I love him and I want him to get better. I need him to get past this. He isn't doing well, and I'm worried."

"He misses Nadia," Caitlin said. "We all do."

Lori-Anne sat back in her chair. "Uncle Mathieu is in a bad place. He's really depressed, and not in a oh-I'm-depressed-to-day-because-I-can't-watch-my-favorite-TV-show, but in a real clinical way, and I'm afraid."

"Why?"

Lori-Anne glanced at her mother. "Because people who are depressed can do desperate things."

"Like what?" Caitlin said.

Lori-Anne hesitated. "I think you know what."

After a long pause, Caitlin said, "Is there anything I can do to help?"

"I have no idea," Lori-Anne said. "I just don't know."

CB ⅏

Mathieu heard a car door slam and turned to see his father-in-law walking toward him. The old man laboured up the driveway and Mathieu noticed how old Samuel suddenly looked. Didn't make him seem as imposing or intimidating. Although Samuel's intimidation had never worked on Mathieu, possibly because Mathieu was the same height and a bit heavier than Samuel. And now he had youth on his side too.

"What the hell are you doing here?" Mathieu said and put the rag he'd been using to apply Danish Oil to parts of the bed down on the workbench. "I'm really not in the mood for your bull-shit."

"I thought maybe we could talk," Samuel said.

Mathieu grabbed a clean rag and wiped his hands. "About?"

Samuel licked his lips a few times. "Working on such a beautiful day?"

"Why are you here?" he said. "I'm sure it's not to shoot the crap."

Samuel cleared his throat.

"I suppose you're right about that," he said. "You and Lori aren't doing too good these days."

"No shit, Sam," Mathieu said, taking a step forward. "In case you haven't been paying attention, we lost our only child."

"She was my granddaughter—"

"And how often did you spend time with her?"

Samuel took a step back. "Huh?"

"In the fourteen years she was alive, how many damn times did you spend with her? Did you know anything about her?"

"We had her over to our place plenty of times—"

"Oh sure, at Christmas, Easter, big family gatherings," Mathieu said, taking another step forward. "But did you spend any time with her?"

"I'm sure I did."

"Name one time."

Samuel opened his mouth then closed it. "Look, that's not why I came over."

"Why did you come?" Mathieu said, taking another step forward. "Lori-Anne isn't here if that's who you're looking for."

"You and I, we've never quite seen eye-to-eye."

"That's all your doing. You've never liked me."

"That's not it," Samuel said. "I simply never thought you were right for Lori. I'd expected more from her."

"So I was a big disappointment to you. Didn't live up to Sam Weatherly's high standards."

"I wanted Lori to take over for me . . ."

"And because of me you had to settle for Jim. What? He's not living up to your expectations either? Maybe your expectations are set a little too high. You ask me, that's a recipe for disappointment."

Samuel rubbed his lips with his hand. "Look, I'm not a bad guy. I worked hard and provided for my family. Gave them all a fair chance. I grew up pretty poor so I know what it's like to have nothing."

"Yeah, I know. You're a self-made man who seems to look down on other people. Why is that? You think you're better than the rest of us?"

"No, no I don't. I'm sure you find that hard to believe. I just wanted my kids to have what I didn't. I wanted them to know that hard work gets rewarded."

"Hard work does, but showing love is also important."

Samuel looked like he'd been slapped. "I love them all, even Cory."

"When's the last time you told any of them, especially Cory."

Samuel made a dismissive hand gesture. "I'm sure they know."

"I'm sure they don't."

An uncomfortable silence settled between them. Mathieu rubbed his hands with the clean rag like he was trying to remove something that wasn't there.

"I have a proposition."

"A proposition?"

Samuel nodded. "Yes."

"So talk," Mathieu said when his father-in-law said nothing more. "I have work to do."

"I'd like to offer you a settlement."

"Is this some kind of a joke?"

Samuel shook his head. "Starting over takes money."

"Wow," Mathieu said. "I never expected that, not even from you. You really think money is the answer?"

"It helps."

"Won't help bring Nadia back."

Samuel looked like he'd been slapped again, but only for a second.

"Lori's not getting anywhere with the way things are between the two of you. I thought if this is going to end in a divorce anyway, why not—"

"Go to hell, you bastard."

"I can make it easier for you to start over. Lori is still young."

"Get off my property."

"I won't offer this again," Samuel said in a low, even-keeled voice. "If you don't take me up on it now, you'll get nothing from me when your marriage ends."

"I don't care," Mathieu said. He grabbed the wet rag and went back to work. "By the way, she hates being called Lori. Guess you don't know your daughter as well as you think you do."

"Think about it."

"Leave," Mathieu said in a tired voice. "If I never see you again, I'll be fine with that."

"This isn't a life for her. You two fighting all the time. She deserves better," Samuel called out from the end of the driveway. "So much better."

Mathieu turned around. "And so does Victoria."

Once his father-in-law was gone, Mathieu put his rag down, sat on a stool, and rested his hands on his thighs to try and calm down. He replayed the scene in his mind, but felt more confused than ever. Had Lori-Anne gone to her parents and told them everything? Had her father really tried to buy him off? Who the hell did that? This wasn't some TV show where shit like that happened.

Mathieu stood and paced. If Lori-Anne wanted a divorce, why didn't she just ask? No, he didn't think she did, not yet anyway. This was purely the old man getting his nose into someone else's business. Mathieu's business. What an arrogant SOB. Had he really believed that Mathieu could be bought?

"Hi Uncle Mathieu."

"Jesus!" he said. "Scared the you-know-what out of me."

"Sorry," Caitlin said as she stepped off her bike and put it down on the driveway. "What are you doing?"

"I was taking a break."

Caitlin walked into the garage. "That's the bed for that girl? Looks really nice."

"Thanks," he said. "It's turned out pretty good."

"All the things you make do."

He smiled. "That's because you've never seen the things that go wrong. I usually trash those and start over."

"Really?"

He nodded. "People pay me good money for custom furniture, so I can't give them anything but the best."

"I guess," she said and ambled over to his workbench. He watched her look at a few tools. "I saw Aunt Lori-Anne this morning. At Grandma's."

"You did?"

Caitlin nodded. "I went to see Grandma because I was mad at my parents and I knew Dad wanted to take me for the day and I didn't want to be with him and his new girlfriend so I went to Grandma's."

Mathieu didn't say anything.

"Aunt Lori-Anne was mad at you."

"I know." He paused and looked at his niece. "I just can't seem to do the right thing by your aunt lately."

"That's because you're still hurting from losing Nadia."

Mathieu watched her take a chisel in her hands and was glad he'd put the cap on the cutting end. "It is, but it doesn't make it right to hurt your aunt. I need to be better."

"If Nadia was here, do you think you and Aunt Lori-Anne would be fighting?"

"No, we wouldn't be."

"So all you have to do is pretend."

"It's not that simple," he said. "That's one pain I can't pretend doesn't exist. Nadia was my special little girl."

"I wish my dad thought of me that way," she said. "I don't think he does. He's never spent a lot of time with me. Not like you did with Nadia and me. You're more of a dad to me than he is. Maybe I should come and live with you guys."

"Caitlin." Mathieu waited for her to look at him. "You have a home. Your mother loves you and I'm sure your dad does too even if he doesn't live there anymore. And you can't take Nadia's place."

"I know," she said. "It's just maybe if I . . ."

"What?"

"Well, Aunt Lori-Anne said you're really depressed because you miss Nadia so much and you guys are always fighting, and I thought maybe if I was here, it would be like . . . better."

Mathieu looked at nothing in particular so he could sort out his thoughts.

"You're a wonderful, thoughtful young lady," he said. "And I love you for wanting to help. But I need to find peace in my own heart about Nadia. I can't have my niece take her place. That would be so . . ."

"Weird."

"Yeah. It would. It sure would." He thought back to Samuel's unexpected visit. The old man had wanted to ruin his marriage and his life, and here was his fourteen-year-old niece doing exactly the opposite. "I think your dad is missing out on a great kid."

Her face lit up and once again he saw the family resemblance. It made him look away.

"You love Aunt Lori-Anne?"

He forced himself to look at Caitlin. "Yeah, I really do."

She smiled. "That's good."

Mathieu smiled back. "Yes, I think it is."

"Well, I guess I should go home," Caitlin said. "Before my mom reports me as a missing person." She got on her bike. "See ya."

"Be careful," Mathieu said. "And tell your mom I say hi."

"I will."

Mathieu watched her ride down the driveway, cross the road, and disappear from sight.

CS ∞

Lori-Anne and her mother sat outside at the patio table after Caitlin left, drinking iced tea and talking. Mostly, Lori-Anne talked and Victoria listened. Lori-Anne didn't hold anything back. She was tired of hoping that things were going to get better when it was obvious they weren't. She'd been denying too many things lately.

Lori-Anne told her mother about Mathieu's mood swings, the way he walked with his shoulders rounded and his head hung low as if the weight of all his grief was too much to bear. He had dark and lifeless eyes, like the real Mathieu was lost somewhere behind those eyes and there was no way to reach him. He was unpredictable, either sad and helpless, or granite hard and ready to fight. They hadn't slept in the same bed for weeks, and never ate together. They spoke, when they spoke at all, with cutting cordiality. Even her work no longer provided refuge. How could she heal when she spent her days wondering what he might do?

"Maybe it's time for me to face reality and accept that we're not going to get through this."

"Oh, honey, it's not that bad."

"It feels like it, mom. I thought I could handle anything, but . . ."

Lori-Anne looked out into the yard, the calm pool water a contrast to the turmoil inside of her. She couldn't remember the last time she'd felt at peace.

"You'll be fine," Victoria said. "I have faith in you."

"Glad someone does."

"Did you mean what you said earlier to Caitlin, about Mathieu blaming you?"

Lori-Anne shrugged. "Wouldn't that make it easier if he did say it? Wouldn't that be easier on him, like a burden tossed away? I'm not without blame. I was driving and I was distracted."

"You need to stop torturing yourself if you expect to help your husband," Victoria said. "Maybe you want him to blame you because you feel you deserve to be blamed?"

"Maybe I do," Lori-Anne said and put her fist to her mouth so she could bite down on her fingers. "If it wasn't for me—"

"Stop! Maybe Mathieu isn't the only one unable to move forward."

"I want us to get help, not just him. I need to tell him, but I can't. I want him to hold me and tell me it wasn't my fault." Lori-Anne snatched a couple of tissues from the tissue box her mother had had the good sense to bring out with them. She wiped her eyes and blew her nose. "But he can't tell me that because it really was my fault."

"We all make mistakes."

"Except mine killed my daughter."

"It wasn't your fault. It was an accident."

Lori-Anne shook her head so hard her hair whipped across her face. "Maybe it's me that's preventing him from moving on. Maybe if he didn't see me every day, he wouldn't be reminded of what I did. Maybe he'd be better off without me."

"I don't think so."

"Why not?"

"Because he loves you, I know he does."

"You can't know that."

"He's a good man. You know that. You wouldn't have married him otherwise. Keep that in mind. He's in a world of pain and he's not seeing things right. He'll come around."

"How can you be so sure?"

"Just look at his grandfather," Victoria said. "Mathieu is so much like him, but he's still young. And grief can blind us and make us forget what's important. You are important to him, honey. Each day, the pain will ease off a bit. It may take a long time, but don't give up."

"But how long do I have to wait?"

"However long it takes. You go home and keep trying. Giving up on him will not do either one of you any good. Try and do things, however small, that will help him, even if he doesn't see it that way."

"Feels like anything I do is wrong."

"Just do your best."

When Lori-Anne arrived home, she noticed Mathieu's new truck wasn't in the driveway. He'd probably gone to see his grandparents. Inside, the house was uncomfortably quiet. She put her purse, keys, and phone on the hall table and headed to the kitchen to see if he'd left a note.

Nothing. She wasn't really surprised. This was the state of their marriage. Her mother had told her to go home and do something to help him. Maybe she should make dinner, set the table, and they could at least eat together.

Lori-Anne went to the fridge to see if she could find something to turn into a meal, but then her phone beeped three times. She hurried to the foyer and grabbed her cell.

"Oh no," she said after reading the text. "Not now. Damn it!"

She grabbed her purse and keys, and left.

ELEVEN

Canada Day
July 1, 2012
6:41 p.m.

Lori-Anne felt panicky, her throat was closing, and her heart hammered against her ribs. She stopped just outside the emergency room doors, took a couple of deep breaths, and forced herself to enter the hospital. A blast of cold air hit her, a shocking difference from the muggy heat outside.

She rubbed her arms and looked around. The place was crowded and noisy. There was a baby screeching and a mother doing her best to quiet the child; a group of people appearing to be of Middle East origin were talking loudly, huddled over a boy with a bloody face; a black couple, maybe in their early thirties, were trying to soothe a little girl who looked pale and dazed as she lay across the mother's lap.

Lori-Anne couldn't see her husband.

Her mind reeled back to those three small words that could totally destroy the man she loved. How would he handle this on top of losing Nadia? She looked at faces, trying to see who might be going through worse things than they were. But none of these people were here by choice. It didn't matter what tragedy they'd suffered. It didn't make it less heartbreaking because no one had died.

Lori-Anne made her way to the nurses' station and tried to get someone's attention. This place was pandemonium. These nurses didn't get paid enough, she probably earned twice as much as they did, and her actions never saved a life.

A tap on her shoulder.

Mathieu.

He said something but she couldn't hear him. He took her hand and led her away from the triage area and down a hall where it was quieter.

"Are you all right?" she said. A couple of nurses walked by, paying little attention to them. "Mathieu?"

"She's dead," he said. "Grandma is dead."

Three little words.

"I'm so sorry," she said.

"A stroke, worse than the last one. Too much for her to take. Grandpa said she was dead before she hit the floor. They were standing in the kitchen talking, and all of a sudden she got this weird look on her face. She was trying to say something but nothing was coming out and he knew what it was. Before he could get to the phone, Grandma crumpled to the floor like a rag. He tried to catch her but she was too heavy for him and he went down with her."

"Did he get hurt?" Lori-Anne said. "Where is he?"

"He's with Grandma," he said. "In one of those rooms." He gestured with his right hand down the corridor.

"How is he?" she said. "Is he in shock?"

Mathieu shook his head. "He seems fine. Says the Lord felt it was time to bring Grandma home." He curled his fists. "I really hate that religious crap. God has no plan except to torture us."

"Mathieu," she said. "Your grandparents are very religious and you have to respect that."

"I respect it, but I don't believe in it," he said. "Grandma was old and she'd already had a stroke. It's all medical. God had nothing to do with it."

"Well, maybe you can keep that to yourself," she said. "We need to be here for Grandpa. He's going to need us once the shock sets in and he realizes that she's really gone."

Mathieu looked toward the room where his grandmother lay dead. She'd been the mother he'd never had, making sure he was taken care of. She'd taken him to doctors' appointments, met with his teachers, and helped with homework. He owed her so much. "I can't believe she's gone either."

"She's in a better place."

Mathieu turned to Lori-Anne, the muscles around his eyes tightening. "Do you believe that?"

Lori-Anne was non-committal. "I guess. She's not suffering, so that has to count for something. Would you have wanted her to survive and live paralyzed? Grandma was too proud to live that way. She wouldn't have wanted to be a burden."

"No, she wouldn't have wanted that," he said. "But is there really a better place? Seems to me that dead is dead." But then he stopped and remembered what had happened during his Father's Day cemetery visit.

"You okay?"

"Yeah. I was just thinking."

"About what?"

"Nothing. It was nothing. I was just thinking about Nadia, about the short time we had with her, that's all. It just makes me feel . . ."

Lori-Anne looked up at her husband. "Nadia gave us fourteen wonderful years. We are who we are because of her. She was our daughter and we loved her no matter how angry she made us sometimes. But wasn't it worth it? I think it was. I'd rather feel this pain that we're feeling right now than to never have known love the way we loved her. She was our beautiful little girl and her short life was not for nothing."

Mathieu looked away, his heart climbing up his throat.

"Look at me," Lori-Anne said.

Slowly, he did.

"Nadia's life wasn't for nothing. You need to believe that. Just like your grandmother's life wasn't for nothing. It doesn't matter how long or short it is. We all bring something to this world, to the people who matter to us."

He nodded but didn't say anything, the muscles around his lungs closing and squeezing the air out like a burst balloon.

"Are you OK?"

After a moment, he was able to nod. "It just never seems to stop."

"I know," she said. "But we can't lose sight of Grandpa. This is a bigger loss for him. Let's go see how he's doing."

CI &D

When she entered the room, Lori-Anne went straight to Grandpa and hugged him. There was comfort in this old man's arms, a comfort she used to get from Mathieu. She even allowed herself to cry quietly into his shoulder, and when she pulled away, he offered her his handkerchief.

She shook her head and pulled a tissue from her purse. "I'm so sorry. Grandma was such a wonderful lady."

"Can't disagree with you," he said, taking hold of his wife's lifeless hand. "Had some great years together. Sure glad she said yes to me so many years ago. Sure glad she did."

Lori-Anne glanced at Mathieu but he was sitting on a chair by the door, his hands clasped between his knees and his head down.

"Are you OK?" she asked Grandpa.

"I miss her already," he said as his lower lip trembled. "We're both old. Can't live forever, I suppose."

She couldn't fathom what it must be like for him, to lose the woman he'd loved for more than sixty years. He probably couldn't remember life without her. They had suffered so much, too. And yet, they'd remained devoted to their faith, going to church every Sunday. She felt ashamed. She hadn't stepped into a church since Nadia's service almost three months ago. Maybe religion should be a bigger part of her life. She glanced at Mathieu again and knew that it would be a solo journey if she decided to follow through. If he'd had any faith, it was gone now.

Lori-Anne gave Grandpa's arm a rub and he smiled at her. His eyes reminded her of Mathieu's. His jaw was also Mathieu's jaw. She'd seen a picture of Grandpa at Mathieu's age and they looked so alike, they could have been brothers. Words her mother had said came to her: *he's just like his grandfather, a good man with a good heart, just a bit lost right now*. Lori-Anne saw it, the truth of it.

"I remember the first time I met you both," she said. "Mathieu hadn't told me you were his grandparents and I kept thinking, wow, his parents are sort of old, and then I noticed the picture on the small table by the sofa, the picture of Mathieu with a young couple, and stupid me, I asked who they were and you all went quiet for a moment and then Grandma took me aside and told me the whole story. My heart and my love went to Mathieu that night, and to the two of you."

Grandpa smiled and patted her hand. "We were just glad he'd finally brought a girlfriend home, and a pretty and smart one at that."

Lori-Anne blushed.

"Do you want us to take care of things for you?" she said.

"No need," he said. "We made plans a while back, after her first stroke, just in case. We realized we weren't going to be around forever and we didn't want you and Mathieu to be burdened, scrambling to get it all arranged. I just need to make a phone call."

"Guess she'll be buried with the rest of the family."

Grandpa nodded. "There's room for all of us there."

Lori-Anne glanced at her husband, and this time he was looking at her and she could see how overwhelmed he was.

He must feel like his world is imploding, she thought, and there isn't a thing he can do to stop it.

"Going to get something to drink," Mathieu said. "Anyone else want something?"

"A bottle of water would be great," Lori-Anne said.

Once Mathieu had left the room, she said, "You'll let me know if there's anything I can do. Anything at all."

"I think Mathieu needs your help more than I do. I'll be fine. But the boy, he's been through a lot and I'll be honest, I'm worried. And I know you are too, it's written all over your face. Any luck with counselling?"

Lori-Anne shook her head. "I mentioned it the one time and it became a fight," she said. "He's stubborn. Thinks he'll get through it by himself, somehow. But I'm worried. Even more than before, if that's possible. I don't know what losing Grandma is going to do to him."

Grandpa nodded. "I'll keep an eye on him."

"But you have your own loss to deal with."

"I'll be fine."

"Now I know where he gets it from."

"We are a proud bunch," he said with a hint of a grin. "I'll miss my Flore I have no doubt, but I'm more worried about Mathieu. I've never seen him like this."

"It's like something was switched off inside of him."

"That's one way of putting it."

Mathieu came back and they fell silent. He handed Lori-Anne a bottle of water. She took a couple of sips.

"When will you have the service?" she said.

"I have to speak to the funeral director, but maybe Thursday. Give me a chance to let people know. She had a lot of friends at the community centre. Still volunteered once a week."

Lori-Anne looked at Grandma. "She was always thinking of others."

"She was," Grandpa said. "They'll all want to come and say goodbye."

"It's getting late. I'm sure the nurses will be asking us to leave soon." She turned to Mathieu. "You staying?"

"A bit longer. Going to drive Grandpa home."

"Sure," she said.

Lori-Anne kissed Grandpa on the cheek and left without kissing her husband.

TWELVE

July 2, 2012
5:00 a.m.

The five o'clock sun shone through the bedroom window, right into Mathieu's face. He'd slept on Nadia's bed, her stuffed animals helter-skelter around him and on the floor.

He couldn't remember falling asleep.

Shortly after nine the nurses had asked them to leave so that Grandma could be looked after, which Mathieu assumed meant taken to the morgue. His grandfather had left without a fuss, and so had he, feeling small and misplaced. He and Grandpa had walked down the hospital corridor in silence, Mathieu wondering how his grandfather would cope on his own. He'd heard that when a couple had been married for as long as his grandparents had, when one of them went, the other followed shortly after, as if the surviving spouse couldn't live without the other.

He'd driven Grandpa home and made sure his grandfather settled in for the night before heading out. He dimly recalled making his way up the stairs to Nadia's room. He'd probably opened her door like he did every night just to get a sense of her and had sat on her bed and then lay down.

Mathieu pushed himself up, knocking a stuffed frog to the floor where it noiselessly came to rest beside a two-foot-long snake. Lori-Anne had always hated that snake, any snake for that matter, stuffed or real. She had tried to convince Nadia on several occasions that she should get rid of it, but Nadia had refused, finding it funny that her mom was afraid of a toy.

"It's not real, Mom. Get a grip," Nadia would say.

Mathieu had bought that snake in Picton, on the way home from their first camping trip. Nadia had been seven. She'd bugged them that all her friends went camping during the summer and that she was the only one who never had any camping stories to tell come the new school year, so Mathieu bought a tent, air mattresses, sleeping bags, and all the other gear he thought they needed, and they drove to Sandbanks. He'd researched campsites across Ontario and had read so many great comments about that campground. If the best campsite in the province turned out to be a horrible experience, then they could at least say they'd tried it and never go again.

He managed to pack everything into his Honda Civic, the same one his daughter would die in years later, and off they'd gone. It drizzled on the way there, but as they got closer to the site the sky cleared and the temperature shot up ten degrees. Setting up camp took them almost two hours, and by late afternoon, pleased with their efforts, he and Lori-Anne cracked open a couple of drinks and toasted to their first family camping trip.

That's when they realized that Nadia was nowhere to be seen.

They looked inside the tent, around the site, checked the outhouse. They asked other campers if they'd seen a seven-year-old girl, just under four feet tall, long blond hair and blue-grey eyes, wearing white shorts, a pink camisole and a pink baseball cap. No one had seen her. Other parents reassured them that she'd probably made friends—it was so easy when camping to make friends they all said—and that the kids were probably just exploring. It's what kids did when camping.

Forced smiles and stiff thank yous were all they could manage. The idea of losing her nauseated them. Only a few hours into their first camping trip and they were regretting it already. No one had offered to help. No one seemed concerned.

They checked the restrooms and shower facilities. More outhouses. Finally, one camper pointed to an area where kids got together to play. They thanked him and ran, calling out her name a little too loudly.

"Mommy! Daddy!" Nadia ran to them, grinning from ear to ear, brandishing a small field snake as if it were a prized trophy.

Lori-Anne screamed—a scream that carried across the entire campground. The park rangers showed up a few minutes later to make sure no one was being mauled by a bear or some other wild animal. Bears were extremely rare in Sandbanks. Racoons, skunks, and snakes, however, were plentiful.

Mathieu scooped the stuffed animals from the floor and put them on the bed, having no idea how Nadia used to arrange them.

"Sorry, honey," he said, "for messing up your bed."

Oh Daddy, don't you know anything?

He'd heard that plenty of times over the years. She would try to be angry with him, her hands on her hips and a scowl on her face because he'd messed up her stuffed animals, so he'd pick her up and throw her on the bed and tickle her. Her arms would flail and knock the animals all over the place, and then she'd try to be really angry with him but he'd tickle her even more and she would laugh harder and beg him to stop, please, please stop Daddy before I pee my pants, and he would, and then they would sit on the bed, her feet dangling over the edge.

He was so happy at those times, never realizing that someday she would get older and wouldn't want her dad to tickle her that way, wouldn't want to spend time playing dolls with him or board games like Junior Monopoly or the Game of Life. No, he'd never thought that in a few short years she'd be a teenager and he'd be just Dad, not Daddy, and he wouldn't mean as much to her but she would mean just as much to him.

That had happened almost overnight, when she'd turned thirteen. His little girl wasn't so little anymore and she didn't need him as much. He couldn't get used to that. He'd always done so much with her and for her, and now she didn't want him. He didn't know when it was okay to do something for her or when to let her be. He seemed to get it wrong every time, and Nadia got angry with him no matter what.

Every parent had to grind through the teenage years, knowing they wouldn't last forever. With a little hope and luck, their teenager would turn out to be a beautiful, loving, and caring adult. Mathieu thought about the Nadia he would never know, the person she would have grown up to be.

He would have loved to have known that person.

Mathieu sat at her desk and powered up Nadia's laptop. He was on autopilot, not really aware of what he was doing, drawn by Nadia's presence which filled the air, thick and vibrant. In this room she had played with her Barbies, had Caitlin over for sleepovers, danced to music playing on the radio or iPod, taped posters on the walls of Jacob from Twilight and more recently one of Kurt Cobain.

He clicked on the Internet Explorer icon and Facebook came up. Nadia had set it up so that it signed in automatically. Mathieu felt like a voyeur, but he couldn't turn away. There were comments from yesterday, friends saying how much they missed her, how they wished she was still here, that it sucked that she had died.

Yeah, it sucked big time.

He navigated down her Facebook page and stopped when he found some sort of poem.

Why do things hurt so much?
Sometimes, at night, I think I can't
I'm so lonely amongst a thousand friends
Who can't help me get rid of the pain
Why does he ignore me all the time
When he knows I love him so much
I feel like a fool
But can't stop myself no matter
He looks at me but doesn't see

My heart beating so hard for him
I run away to hide my tears
Bury my pain in the shame of my feelings
I hate being like this
It turns my world into a dark place
That just won't see any light
Things I used to love, I now hurt
And can't help doing it
I'm ashamed of it
But can't stop myself

Mathieu stared at the words. It wasn't great writing, but it was honest—painfully honest. Nadia had been in love with some boy who hadn't returned her love. Cliché, yes, but not for a fourteen-year-old. He understood that much. Friends, first crushes, were life and death at that age.

This was a part of his daughter's life he'd known nothing about. Had Lori-Anne? Is that why she'd wanted to drive Nadia to dance that day? If so, why hadn't she shared that with him? Maybe he could have helped, somehow, offered a boy's point of view. And why hadn't Nadia talked to him? She used to tell him everything.

Because you're a dad, and dads don't like their little girls to grow up and fall in love. When she'd been a child, of course it had been easy for her to confide in him. But at fourteen, on the cusp of womanhood?

He looked at the poem again. Something about it bothered him, not the writing, but the posting. His hand touched the screen, his fingertips running over each word, desperate to reach into a past that was simply no longer reachable.

Then he got it.

The time-stamp—March 26, 2012, 4:46.

Everything inside of him turned to mush and he struggled to breathe. He felt paralyzed, he felt anger rise like bile in the back of his throat, he felt like hurling the laptop across the room.

But mostly he felt that the worst day of his life would never end.

THIRTEEN

July 2, 2012
5:52 a.m.

L ori-Anne returned from the bathroom but instead of getting back into bed, she stepped into the hallway, thinking she'd heard a noise. The door to Nadia's room was ajar. She walked toward her daughter's room, hesitated for a second, then pushed the door wide open.

"Mathieu?"

He sat at the little desk he'd built for Nadia about three years ago so she could do her homework in a quiet place instead of down in the kitchen where she was easily distracted. He was staring at the computer screen with wide and haunted eyes, which made her want to sneak back to her room and pretend nothing was happening.

"Mathieu?"

Lori-Anne closed her eyes. The weariness of it all drained her. It would be much easier to simply walk away. At some point, she needed to think of her sanity and well-being. Yes, her mother had told her to be patient, that Mathieu was a good man who was lost. But how long before she lost herself trying to save him?

How long?

"Mathieu?" she said again. Three months since her daughter's death and Lori-Anne still couldn't step into Nadia's room. Maybe she was as messed up as her husband. Maybe she was the one who needed counselling. "Mathieu?"

This time, he turned to look at her.

"What are you doing? You're shaking. What's wrong?" She hoped she sounded concerned instead of annoyed.

He waved her in.

"Just tell me," she said.

"Christ, Lori-Anne," he said. "You still won't come into her room."

"Never mind," she said. "Just tell me what's got you so freaked out."

He looked back at the computer screen, and Lori-Anne thought he wasn't going to tell her.

"D'you know what she was doing in the car that day?"

"What are you talking about?"

"The day of the accident."

"I get that," she said. "But what are you talking about? I was trying to talk to her, get her to open up."

"Did she say anything?"

"Did she ever?" Lori-Anne said. "You know she was difficult."

"So you talked and she listened but said nothing."

Lori-Anne rolled her eyes. "Something like that."

"Was she on her phone?"

"No, she wasn't talking to anyone. Like I said, I was trying to get her to talk."

"Yeah, but was she texting?"

"Yes, and it was annoying me," she said. "I wanted her to tell me what was going on. And I was trying to keep my eyes on the road."

Mathieu made a snorting sound. "Little good that did."

"Fuck you, Mathieu," she said. "I'm so damn tired of you blaming me for that accident. It happened. Could have been you instead of me. It could have happened to anyone. It just so happens that it happened to us. Don't you think I have to live with this my entire life now? Don't you think I replay the accident every day, wishing I'd done something different, left a few minutes earlier or later, taken a different route, stopped for gas, so things could have ended differently? But you know what? I can't change the past. And neither can you. I know you blame me but no amount of blame will change anything."

He said nothing.

"You need to let that go," she said. "Or d'you enjoy having us like this? Is that it? You like the way our marriage is? You like being miserable all the time? You like drowning in self-pity? You like making me feel guilty?"

Mathieu opened his mouth to say something, and then closed it.

"Talk to me," she said. "Why can't you just talk to me? Quit shutting me out and talk to me. I'm willing to get counselling for us so we can work through this. Don't you want things to get better?"

"What if they can't?"

"We have to try."

"But . . ." He turned to the computer screen again.

"What's so interesting on that laptop?" she said. "Just tell me."

"You have to see this. Come here."

Lori-Anne let out a heavy sigh. She didn't have the energy to keep fighting, so she finally crossed the imaginary line that had kept her out of her daughter's room all these months.

And she felt it instantly—the closeness to their daughter. Nadia's presence assaulted Lori-Anne, coming from everywhere: the curtains, the bedspread, the clothes in her closet, the books on the bookshelf, the iPod on the night table, the laptop on the desk.

Nadia was gone but her room emanated this overwhelming aura. In here, Nadia was still alive.

This wasn't good. No wonder Mathieu couldn't let go, no wonder he spent so much time here. The room had to be cleaned. No, more than that. It needed a thorough cleansing. But it felt sacrilegious to erase the last reminder of their daughter. Besides, Mathieu would never allow it. If she went behind his back, it would be the end of their marriage.

Her shoulders sagged. She didn't want to fight anymore. It drained her and didn't solve a thing. All she wanted was to fall into his arms, feel the warmth of him, smell his scent, and connect with him like they used to.

But did he want her? She thought of the way he blew up at her all the time, his eyes stormy and full of ire, making her step back as if she'd been scorched. That wasn't the man who had vowed to love her forever.

"What do you need me to see so bad?" she said and came closer to him.

"This," he said, pointing at the screen.

Lori-Anne looked at what appeared to be some sort of poem or song, and shrugged. "So?"

"This is Nadia's Facebook page."

She looked a little closer. "And?"

"Did you read it?"

"Well, no," she said. "What are you getting at? So she wrote something on her Facebook page. All the kids do that. Probably doesn't mean anything to us."

"She was in love, did you know that?"

"In . . . love?"

"Yeah," he said. He read the poem aloud to her.

"Okay," she said. "She was a teenager. They fall in love by the minute."

"Maybe so," he said. "Look at the posting time."

"Oh my God! No wonder she didn't want to give me her phone. She was uploading this to her Facebook when it happened." A chill ran through her. "I . . . can't believe this."

"She's gone but this poem is captured forever. So weird."

"That's a day I wish had never happened."

They both stared at the computer screen, saying nothing.

"Our little girl was in love with a jerk, apparently," Mathieu said to break the silence. "She had a broken heart. Could be why she'd become so moody."

"I guess."

"Whoever he was didn't return her love. It's obvious by her words."

"Maybe that wasn't such a bad thing," she said. "Not like we were going to let her date at fourteen."

"I know," he said. "But she was hurt."

"For all we know he was a senior who didn't even know her."

"True."

Lori-Anne sat on the edge of the bed, her shoulders caving in. Nadia's absence was so overwhelming in her room. Now more than ever, she wanted to clean it.

"So what do we do now?" she said in a voice that had no energy.

"Print it," he said. "This is the very last moment on earth our daughter had."

"No, not about that. About us." She ran a hand across her forehead.

"She died while posting this," he said. "It's almost like being with her."

"NO!" she said, getting to her feet. "It's not. I was there and it was horrible. When the car got sandwiched, it sounded like a thousand pop cans being crushed. Glass exploded and I heard Nadia scream. I'll never get those sounds out of my head. I'll never get the guilt out of my soul."

Lori-Anne stopped. She wanted to tell him what Nadia had said just before the crash, but he wasn't listening, he wasn't getting it, he wasn't trying to comfort her. Instead, he stared at the computer.

She felt like spitting in his face.

Lori-Anne left the room without saying a word and hurried to her bedroom where she threw herself on the bed like a child.

That's how small she felt.

Or how big the situation had become.

She curled up, looking for some sort of comfort that might chase away the hopelessness and helplessness that consumed her. She didn't know what to do, how to reach him. She had lost a daughter and was now losing a husband.

Her husband.

Who was he? Who had he become? What exactly did they share now? Seemed like nothing. So how could she share the last moment of Nadia's life with him?

God, she needed to. The burden of carrying Nadia's words had become too much. Those words, Nadia's last words, were just too difficult to voice. Children often said things they didn't mean, and parents could dismiss what they said and move on, but Lori-Anne couldn't do that. Her daughter was gone. Nadia would never say another thing to her mother that would amend her dying words. Lori-Anne had to live with the sting of those words, a dirty secret that burned like an eternal punishment.

☙ ❧

"Nadia, I'm talking to you. Can you please put your phone away? Are you listening to me?"

Silence.

"Gimme the phone."

"No, I'm doing something."

"This is the attitude I want to discuss with you. And your poor grades."

"They're fine."

"No, they're not. Gimme the phone."

"It's my phone."

"That we pay for so if I want to take it away, I will. Are you doing drugs?"

"I'm just a kid having fun. I know growing up with Granddad you didn't get to have fun, but that's not my problem. I'm not like you, work, work, work."

"School is important."

"I'm only fourteen."

"Nadia, gimme the phone."

"No."

Nadia types really fast on her phone.

"Damnit, Nad. Gimme the phone so you can pay attention to what I'm saying."

Lori-Anne grabs it.

"Hey, give it back. I wasn't done posting—"

"Posting what?"

"Never mind. I hate you."

CঙৎO

Those words, cold and spoken with a sharp tongue, slashed Lori-Anne's heart. No matter how hard she tried to tell herself that Nadia had needed to lash out at someone, anyone (because she'd been in love with a boy who hadn't returned her feelings, Lori-Anne now knew), those words, the very last words her daughter had spoken to her, hurt almost as much as missing her did.

That's what she'd wanted to tell Mathieu. She needed to hear him say that Nadia hadn't meant it, that she'd apologize if she could. She needed Mathieu to be her strength so that, for once, she could put aside her bravado and be comforted.

Was that so much to ask?

Why couldn't he do that, be the strong one?

Why was he punishing her?

Yes, punishing her.

She hadn't done anything wrong. She'd just wanted to talk to their daughter because she was concerned and worried. Any good parent would have done the same. Any caring mother would have done the same. She knew that Mathieu would have done the same.

It was an accident. A dumb, stupid car accident.

Lori-Anne curled into a ball. She was tired, so tired. Physically and emotionally. But mostly, she was tired of being alone.

FOURTEEN

July 2, 2012
11:33 a.m.

ori-Anne woke feeling groggy. She turned and glanced at the clock. Crap! It was after eleven. She was late for work! No, wait a minute. Since Canada Day, yesterday, had fallen on a Sunday, she didn't have to work today. Good. Perfect. She was in no shape for that anyway.

She rolled over and closed her eyes. The confrontation with Mathieu came back to her. All its ugliness, all its pain, all its unsolved issues. It was giving her a headache. He was giving her a headache. And that room, Nadia's bedroom, she had to do something about that. It creeped her out being in there and feeling so much of her daughter. No wonder Mathieu couldn't let go and move forward.

Lori-Anne bounced out of bed and went to find Mathieu. She'd had enough. Nothing about their situation was healthy. Since he was unwilling to get help, like her mother had said to her, she should do things to help him along and the way she saw it, Nadia's room wasn't going to be a shrine another day.

She couldn't find him, not in his office, not in their daughter's room, not in the workshop. She finally found a note on the kitchen counter, beside the empty fruit bowl: *Gone to Grandpa's.*

Lori-Anne's shoulders sagged. How could she have forgotten? Poor Grandpa. She should call him. Make sure he was OK. No. Not right now. She needed to stick to her plan, especially since Mathieu was out of the house. He was with his grandfather so Lori-Anne didn't need to worry that Grandpa was alone. She'd do what she needed to do and then call Grandpa.

She made a pot of coffee, filled the biggest mug she could find and headed up to Nadia's room. She crossed the threshold and instantly her daughter's presence wrapped itself around her, like a warm hug. Her legs turned to water and for a moment she second-guessed herself. But instead of leaving, she shut her eyes and waited for the moment to pass. Then she put her cup on the desk, opened the window to let all the bad vibes escape, shoved the stuffed animals off the bed, and stripped it.

She threw the sheets out into the hallway. Next, Lori-Anne attacked the closet. She pulled out a skirt Nadia hadn't worn in three years. It was purple and too small. She chucked it on the bed.

A white blouse.

Chuck.

Old sweatpants with frayed hems.

Chuck.

Sweatshirts from the dance studio that Nadia didn't wear.

Chuck.

Skinny jeans that showed way too much.

Chuck.

T-shirts with Justin Bieber on them.

Chuck.

Long-sleeved T-shirts from West 49.

Chuck.

A fall jacket that Nadia had barely worn. Lori-Anne recalled going from store to store at the mall before finding that jacket. Nadia had been thrilled, but then only wore it a few times. Maybe someone at school had made fun of it and Nadia's feelings had been hurt. Kids could be mean.

Chuck.

She went through the entire closet, throwing everything onto the bed. Some of her things were good enough to donate to the Diabetes Association or the Salvation Army. The real old and worn things were going in the trash.

Next she tackled the dresser. Old undies, socks, pajamas, shorts, and tired-looking T-shirts of different sizes and colours piled up on the bed. There were clothes here from when she was eight or nine, things she couldn't fit into even if she'd still wanted to wear them. That task had gotten away from them. They kept buying new but never tossed out the old. Today everything was going.

Chuck, chuck, chuck.

Lori-Anne was on a roll. Over an hour had passed and she had a mountain on the bed. She ran down to the garage to grab a few green garbage bags. She put the good stuff into a separate pile and filled three bags, trying to keep the clothes somewhat folded so they wouldn't look all frumpy later. She got some masking tape and a marker from the kitchen drawer and wrote D.A. on two bags and S.A. on the third and brought them down to the basement. She would call for a pickup date tomorrow. Another two bags she jammed full of clothes labelled as garbage.

When that was done, she looked at what else she could get rid of. Nadia had thirty or forty books on her bookshelves, posters all over her walls, CDs that she hadn't listened to since ripping them to her iPod.

She went looking for boxes. They usually had a few in the garage. All she found were two filled with Mathieu's supplies which she emptied and left on his workbench. He could sort that out later. Back in Nadia's room, she filled the boxes with books. Maybe she could donate them to the library. They were all in great shape. She pulled Kurt Cobain's poster off the wall, rolled it and squeezed it between books in the box. She did the same with the three Jacob posters.

She stopped and took a breath. She undid her ponytail, ran both hands through her hair, and redid her ponytail. A lose strand bothered her so she did the whole thing again.

Lori-Anne surveyed the room. It didn't look like a shrine anymore, didn't feel like one either. It just looked like a room no one lived in. She felt tired. The time on the clock radio told her she'd been at it for two hours. Enough for now. The rest would have to wait. She looked at the boxes but they were heavy and she didn't feel like carting them down to the garage. She left them where they were, by the half-empty bookcase.

She sat on the edge of the bed and ran the back of her hand across her sweaty forehead. When Mathieu came home, he'd freak. She was in so much trouble. She'd let her momentum carry her, acting without thinking. It had seemed like the right thing to do. No, it was the right thing to do. If not for him, then for her. All these months, she'd been unable to come into Nadia's room, walking by the closed door day after day like it was some forbidden place. In way, it had been. Her denial had kept her out. If she didn't go in Nadia's room, then she could pretend that Nadia wasn't completely gone. In so many ways, she'd been no better than her husband. But no more. Today, finally, her healing could begin.

And she hoped that Mathieu's could begin too.

She turned, thinking she'd heard the front door open. She waited, holding her breath, steeling herself for the fight that was sure to come. She'd done this for his own good. She needed to remember that.

But she didn't hear any footsteps coming up the stairs. She exhaled but her breath caught in her throat when she heard a car door slam. She hurried to the window but it was just the neighbour across the street.

She needed to take a shower. She needed a glass of wine. She needed to unwind.

Lori-Anne walked away from the window and stopped. It was gone. Nadia's aura was gone. Once again she reasoned that she'd had no other choice, that for them to survive this tragedy, they had to let go of their daughter. But it wasn't easy and she felt her heart close like a little girl's hand.

FIFTEEN

T he house Mathieu had lived in growing up, his grandparents' house, was in Orleans, on the east side of Ottawa. He remembered coming here after the death of his parents and feeling uncomfortable at first, not really knowing his grandparents except for the short visits a few times a year. He hadn't wanted to be there. But his grandmother had been so good and loving, helping him through those horrible first few months, and what he remembered most now was that his childhood had been filled with warmth, love, and plenty of fun times. He could almost hear his grandmother puttering in the kitchen, humming while she baked pies and made wonderful meals, or calling out to him to come and get the garbage bag and take it to the garage. He could hear her throaty laugh filling the house when she was watching one of her TV shows. The small bungalow had always felt just a bit too small, but today it felt big and empty without her.

Mathieu went to the kitchen and took an apple from the crisper and devoured it. Then he cracked open a can of Coke and downed half of it. He heard his grandfather, who had fallen asleep on the sofa chair a while back, stir.

"Mathieu? You still here?"

"Yeah, in the kitchen," he said and walked back to the living room at the front of the house. "I thought I'd let you catch a few winks. You probably didn't sleep much last night."

"I did have a hard time settling down without your grandmother here. That'll take getting used to."

Mathieu drank his Coke. "Will you be all right?"

Grandpa stood and stretched. "I'll miss her. I'm sure some nights will be harder than others. But I'll be fine."

"How can you be so sure?"

"I don't have a choice, now do I? Your grandmother, God rest her soul, is with the good Lord now and not much I can do about it."

"Aren't you angry, even a bit?"

"I'm angry that I won't see her every day, sure, but angry at God? No. He gave her, us, a good long life."

"He took so much from you though."

Grandpa looked at his grandson. "I know where you're trying to get to, but you won't get there with me. For every test that He put in front of us, we did our best, we kept our faith. In the end, that's what He's testing us on. Our love and our faith."

Mathieu frowned. "I don't see it that way."

"I know you don't, son. Can't make you believe something you've closed your mind to."

"He took my parents and my little girl. Not sure what sort of faith I'm supposed to show Him. Not a big fan of His methods."

"Maybe you should come to church with me on Sunday."

Mathieu shook his head. "Thanks, but I'll pass."

"It might help you let go of your anger."

"Maybe my anger is what keeps me going."

"And maybe it's holding you back."

"I don't think so."

"Sometimes, we just have to accept what is and go on. Your grandmother is gone but I'll always have sixty years of memories to keep me company."

"You can't hold memories, tell them you love them, have them tell you they love you too."

"No, you can't. But torturing yourself isn't going to bring your daughter back. Her memories can guide you forward but they shouldn't keep you hostage. And you shouldn't keep Lori-Anne hostage either."

"What did she tell you?"

"Nothing that I can't figure out for myself. Your marriage is in trouble, anyone can see that. It's time to let Nadia rest in peace, like I'll be doing with your grandmother, and pick up your life. You lost your daughter and if you don't smarten up, you'll lose your wife too."

Mathieu put his empty Coke can on the coffee table. "Sorry, Grandpa, I don't want to pick a fight with you. Certainly not after Grandma just died, but maybe that's my business."

"You're my only grandchild, and I love you but I see a man who needs help, in the worst way. I see a wife who keeps trying but is looking rather beaten. You need to talk to her. If you can't talk to her, then the two of you need to see someone who can help."

"So now you're ganging up on me too about the stupid counselling?"

"I'm just trying to make you see what you can't see. Son, I don't like where you're headed. I think it's time to get help."

ᏣᏲ

Mathieu kept to the speed limit and took the long way home, stopping for gas even though he had half a tank left. He was trying to digest his grandfather's words before he got home and faced Lori-Anne, words that wouldn't leave him alone because he knew there was a lot of truth to them. The one thing his grandfather couldn't know though was how hard it had become to forgive Lori-Anne.

They wouldn't be in this predicament if it wasn't for her careless driving. It's not like he was looking for just any reason to blame her. He really didn't want to blame her. But no matter how he looked at what had happened, it was hard not to blame her.

But he wasn't without blame either. Maybe if he'd paid attention that day he would have noticed the snow beginning to fall and told her to take the Pathfinder instead of his car. Things like that he was usually right on top of, but he'd been so into his work that he hadn't noticed the weather. He'd just been thankful Lori-Anne had come home early to take Nadia so that he could get another couple of hours work done. So, he was partially to blame, but he hadn't been the one behind the wheel.

Mathieu pulled into the driveway and saw that Lori-Anne's car was gone. Relief made him exhale the breath he'd been holding. He still wasn't sure what he would say to her but for now he needn't worry. Maybe by the time she came home things would be clearer.

He stepped out of the truck and glanced at the overgrown shrubs. The lawn could also use a cut. Chores he'd tended to like clockwork in the past had slipped his mind lately. The day wasn't too far along, maybe he'd go change into his work clothes and spend a couple of hours doing yard work. Didn't sound like a bad idea.

Mathieu wiggled his key in the front door lock, the humidity making it stick. He'd have to put a little WD40 in it. He put his key ring on one of the hooks by the front door, beside the key that used to be Nadia's. He forced himself to look away then headed for the kitchen. A growl in his stomach was supported by the clock on the stove which indicated it was 5:44. He'd have a quick bite to eat before getting to his chores.

The kitchen was spotless. There was a bit of coffee in the carafe but otherwise the granite counters were bare and there were no dirty dishes in the sink. Mathieu cracked the fridge door open and peeked inside. Nothing appealed to him so he settled for scrambled eggs and toast. He took his dinner to the kitchen table and sat down to eat. There was a note tucked under the glass vase sitting in the middle of the table: *I'm so sorry about everything.*

His fork was halfway to his mouth but he stopped and put it down. He pushed his plate away, his appetite suddenly gone. He took the piece of paper in his hand and read each word. The note made him feel uneasy, like a cold hand around his throat.

He was pretty sure Lori-Anne had gone to her parents. But now he wondered if it was just to clear the air or if she was gone for good?

I'm so sorry about everything.

There was something definitive about those words, almost *goodbye*-like. He didn't like it. He had to talk to her, find out what was going on. He knew he'd been difficult, more like impossible, to live with over the last few months, but it had never occurred to him that Lori-Anne would leave.

I'm so sorry about everything.

Mathieu pulled his cell phone out and dialed Lori-Anne's number. He hesitated before pressing the send button. Maybe he should go over there. No, he couldn't bear to see his father-in-law, especially after the old man's visit.

Just then the grandfather clock bonged six times, reminding him of Samuel. Mathieu got off his chair so fast that it toppled over. He grabbed the clock in a bear hug and carried it out to the garage, not noticing the two garbage bags by the door, and dropped it onto the cement floor, shattering the glass.

"Here's to you, Sammy boy."

Mathieu went back in the house and picked up the kitchen chair. He grabbed his phone and texted Lori-Anne.

What do you mean by your note?

It took a couple of minutes before he got a text back, long enough that he started to worry about how mad she'd be when she saw the grandfather clock.

About what I did.

The accident could have happened to anyone.

True. But that's not it.

I don't understand.

You will. Just know that I thought it would help.

You don't make sense.

I know.

Are you coming home?

Ask me later.

What does that mean?

You'll see.

I guess you're at your parents'?

Yes. How's Grandpa?

Better than me.

It's a different loss.

Maybe, but I'm sure it still hurts.

Of course. But I think he might have been expecting it, especially since Grandma's first stroke.

I guess.

No other text came back right away. He stared at his cold eggs. His stomach grumbled but he was too wound up to eat.

Aren't you coming home?

Ask me later.

You keep saying that.

I'm sorry. I just don't think I can right now. I've done things I'm not sure you can forgive me for. Bye.

The conversation was over. He stared at his phone but no other text came. She couldn't come home and kept apologizing, but why?

He got up, threw the eggs in the compost bin and put his glass of milk in the fridge for later. He stared out the kitchen window into the backyard. The play structure had outlived Nadia. It didn't seem right. He remembered how he and Grandpa had built it over an April weekend when his daughter was just a couple of months old. Lori-Anne and Grandma had made burgers for lunch. He could see Nadia's smiling face when she was about fifteen months and he'd pushed her on the swing for the first time.

The mood to do yard work was gone. Maybe he'd go up to his office and look at pictures of Nadia for a while. It would be nice to see her beautiful smiling face.

Mathieu laboured up the stairs. When he reached the top, he looked back down. He could partially see into the living room where the grandfather clock had been. He had no idea how he was going to explain that to Lori-Anne. The moment had seized him and before he realized it, the grandfather clock was trashed. She'd be pissed with him for a while. Not much he could do about it now.

He turned and saw that Nadia's bedroom door was wide open. He was sure he'd left it closed. He always left it closed and Lori-Anne never went in.

I'm so sorry about everything.

He took a couple of steps on liquid legs.

Just know that I thought it would help.

Mathieu stood in the doorway. His jaw muscles twitched and he felt his anger slam hard against his rib cage. "Lori-Anne," he said between clenched teeth. "Lori-Anne, what have you done?"

He stepped into Nadia's room and felt nothing. He surveyed her room and there was a sick feeling down in his lower stomach, like someone had kicked him in the balls. Everything that had defined his little girl was gone. There was nothing left. Nadia was completely gone.

Lori-Anne had taken his daughter away a second time.

How could she do that?

Why would she do that?

He could never forgive Lori-Anne now.

Mathieu left the room, closed the door gently, and walked down to his office. He sank into his high-backed leather chair, grabbed the mouse, and started looking at pictures of his daughter. There were thousands on his computer.

That was fine, he had all night.

SIXTEEN

July 2, 2012
6:42 p.m.

ori-Anne and Victoria were out on the patio, dark clouds chasing away what had been a beautiful summer's day. The top of the old red maple was bending at a good ten degrees and the lilac bushes shook hard. The water in the pool looked like someone big had just performed the perfect cannonball.

"Everything OK?" Victoria said.

"I don't know." Lori-Anne's focus shifted to the threatening sky. "I might have created the perfect storm at home."

"Don't beat yourself with guilt," Victoria said. "It had to be done at some point."

"But is three months long enough?"

Victoria made a non-committal gesture. "I really can't answer that. You felt that you were ready. Mathieu might never be."

A gust of wind whipped Lori-Anne's hair into her face. She tried to tuck it behind her ears. "I'm so afraid of that. What if he's never ready? How long am I supposed to wait?"

"I don't know."

"Me either," Lori-Anne said, feeling a rain drop. She grabbed her glass of iced tea and her phone. "We should head in. It's getting nasty."

"I so hate to be chased indoors in the summer," Victoria said. "Winters are long enough."

Victoria grabbed the pitcher of iced tea and bowl of nacho chips and the two women settled at the kitchen table just as the rain started to come down in a steady stream. There was a sudden flash in the sky and a low rumble.

"Just in time," Lori-Anne said. "That seemed to come out of nowhere." She grabbed her glass but didn't drink from it. "We never know when it's going to pour down on us, do we?"

Victoria nodded.

"Oh Mom, I never thought it would get so difficult." She put the glass down.

"No one does," Victoria said. "Some have it better and some have it worse. It's never perfect. How we handle the good and the bad is what matters."

Another flash followed closely by a loud bang. "Jesus, that was close." Lori-Anne stared at the rain blurring the patio door. "I don't know if Mathieu can forgive me."

"You know, you might need to forgive yourself first. You're carrying your guilt like a burden."

"I killed my daughter."

"No. No you didn't. It was an accident."

Lori-Anne's eyes met her mother's, and she knew her mom meant well, but in the pit of her stomach, a pool of acid spun around. She'd let her husband and daughter down. How could she not feel guilty about that?

"Seems too easy to hide behind that."

"You're not hiding. You just happened to be at the wrong place at the wrong time. I'm not trying to make light of it, God knows I miss my lovely granddaughter, but it was an accident."

"I just wish my husband would tell me that."

"If you want your husband to forgive you, you need to forgive yourself."

"Even if I do, what about what I did today? What if it pushed him over the edge? I'm worried. He hasn't called or texted. I hope he doesn't do anything stupid."

"I don't think he would."

"Mom, I don't know what he's going to do these days. I really don't. Mathieu's not the man I married. I don't know him anymore, what he's capable of."

"But to hurt himself?"

"I know it seems crazy, but—I don' know. Probably not. I'm just being ridiculous. It's just . . . so much has happened and I guess I expect the worse."

"Oh, honey, it will get better."

"When?"

Victoria shook her head. "You have to believe it will."

"And what if it doesn't?"

"You must have faith."

"I used to," she said. "But lately it just seems really hard. Even a devout Catholic might have her doubts."

"Possibly," Victoria said. "Never hurts to say a Hail Mary or two."

Lori-Anne felt her face tighten as she tried to smile. "I love you Mom. And thanks for trying. I'm just discouraged right now. Can you believe it? Me? Discouraged? You probably never thought you'd hear me say that. I thought I could handle anything, like a good Weatherly. Guess we're not indestructible like Dad thinks we are."

"No, we're not. But we don't give up."

"Not even when the war is lost?"

"It's just a battle. Things will get better."

"And what if they never do?"

"They will."

Lori-Anne's phone buzzed three short times. She looked at the text.

Tell your Dad he's got his wish.

Lori-Anne stared at the message, looked at her mom, then at her phone again.

What are you talking about?

He didn't tell you?

Tell me what?

He wanted to buy me out.

I don't understand.

He came to visit me yesterday.

Why?

To buy me out.

I don't know what you're talking about.

He had a proposition for me. He wanted to give me a settlement.

Are you joking?

I'm not in the mood for jokes.

Why would he do that?

He's never liked me.

That's not true.

Ask him.

Can't believe it.

Believe it.

She didn't know how to respond. He texted her before she could.

Tell him he's got his wish and it won't cost him a penny. I didn't marry you because your family has money. I married you because I loved you.

And you don't anymore?

It's complicated now.

So you don't?

Why did you clean her room?

To save you.

I don't need saving. I need my daughter.

Yes you do because she's not coming back. Please, Matt. Don't do this. It's time to let her go. For your sanity. For our sanity.

I might have forgiven you for the accident, but for what you did today, I can't.

So where does that leave us?

There's no point doing this anymore.

Don't give up.

Why?

Because I still love you. We can fix this.

I don't think we can. Sorry.

Matt, I'm coming over. We can talk about this.

It's too late. I'm tired of this.

So let's fix it.

Lori-Anne waited, thirty seconds, sixty seconds, ninety seconds. She needed to go, she needed to talk to him, she needed to save them. Her phone buzzed just as she was standing. She read the text, each word burning the retina in her eyes and leaving her short of breath as the last twenty years disappeared into a black hole.

I think we should get a divorce.

Lori-Anne tried to mouth the last word but it was so big and full of spurs that it wouldn't pass through her throat. She remembered when she was a teaching assistant and he'd show up to ask her questions that were so off topic that it didn't take long to realize what he was up to. To be fair, she'd kept the charade going for as long as she could, until he finally asked her to go for coffee.

He couldn't give up. He was the one who had chased her. He had made her fall for him. How could he just give up? They needed to talk. They needed to see a marriage counsellor. They didn't need a goddamned divorce.

And what was this about her dad buying him out?

"Honey, what's wrong?" Victoria said.

"Where's Dad?"

"Probably in his study."

Lori-Anne barged in. Her father was sitting behind his desk. "Did you offer Mathieu money to leave me? Did you?"

Samuel closed the book he'd been reading and cleared his throat.

"Answer me, Dad."

"Did he tell you that?"

"Don't play that game with me," she said, slapping the top of his desk. "Don't try to evade the question by asking me questions. You won't fool me. Remember, I learned it from you. Just answer me."

He steepled his fingers and held them in front of his mouth. "He probably misunderstood my intent."

"Come off it, Dad. I'm not stupid."

Samuel got up and approached his daughter. "I was looking after you."

"In case you haven't noticed," she said, "I'm a grown woman and have been taking care of myself for a long time."

"Well, maybe if I'd been more involved, you wouldn't be in this mess."

"And what mess it that?"

"He was never right for you."

Lori-Anne stepped away from her father. "You're back to that. Let it go, Dad. Mathieu is my husband, I love him, you don't have a say in it."

"This situation you're in, if he was the sort of man you need—"

"Stop right there." She waved off further rebuttal with an authoritative hand gesture. "I need him. Not someone else, him. He's my husband. He makes me feel alive, loved, and special."

"Really?" he said. "He's doing that these days?"

1 5 2 | F r a n ç o i s   H o u l e

She pinned him with a cold, raw gaze. "Stay out of this."

"I just want what's best for you."

"No you don't," she said. "You want what's best for you. You want me under your thumb, like Jim. Cory and Brad got away and that really bothered you. And because I'm the only girl you thought you could pull that Daddy dearest crap. Want to know why I had an affair? To get away from you."

"Lori, honey," he said. "You're upset. We should talk about this when you've calmed down."

Anger crossed her face. "You'll never get it. Why you can't accept Mathieu and be happy for me, I'll never understand. He's never done anything but love me. Until recently, we had a really good life together."

"Lori."

"You wanted me to succeed you, because Jim's unpredictable. It wouldn't have mattered who I married, you never would have liked him. You wanted me to run your company because I was safe, you thought I'd do it your way."

"Honey, please—"

"But I didn't want it. I never will, Dad. I love you but what you've done is unforgivable. Mathieu is my husband and I love him. If you can't accept that, then at least respect it."

Lori-Anne turned and saw her mother standing in the doorway.

"I'm sorry, sweetheart," Victoria said.

Lori-Anne hugged her.

"Lori—" Samuel said.

Lori-Anne squared her shoulders. "It's Lori-Anne, Dad. I never liked just Lori. Apparently, something else about me you don't know." She waited a beat to see if he would say anything else but he didn't. She stormed out of the study. "You better hope I can save my marriage, or else—"

She slammed the front door.

SEVENTEEN

July 2, 2012
8:07 p.m.

"Matt? Mathieu?" Lori-Anne called from the foyer, water dripping down her face. It was maybe twenty feet from the driveway to the front door but the rain was coming down hard. "Mathieu?"

She dumped her wet purse on the small table by the front door and took the stairs by two. She made her way down the hall to his office. The door was open. He was sitting at his desk. "Why didn't you answer?"

He shrugged. "Why are you here?"

"Because we need to talk." She wiped her face. "We need to fix this."

"Will it change anything?"

The urge to hit him square in the chin gushed through her veins like hot melted steel. "We won't know unless we try. Matt, this is nuts. We can't just give up. You really want to throw away two decades together?"

His gaze drifted to the window.

"Do you love me?" Her voice sounded high and pleading. "Because I still love you."

"Love doesn't solve everything," he said. "Contrary to what John Lennon sang. Sometimes, we need more than love."

"Then what do we need? What will it take for us to make it work?"

Lori-Anne watched him curl up and shrink into himself. "I don't know."

"Where's the resilient man I know? That young and lovable man who stole my heart? He was romantic and funny and didn't shy away from going after what he wanted. That man believed in us. That man would fight for us. That man would never give up on us."

"That man hadn't lost his daughter," he said. "Things change. Life can do that, beat you down."

"So fight back."

"I'm tired, Lori-Anne. Aren't you? Life's been beating me down since I was six."

"No it hasn't. It wasn't always bad and it won't be forever. We just need to get through this together. Please, Matt, you're not a quitter."

"Maybe your dad is right. Maybe I'm not the man you need."

"I don't believe that."

"It doesn't matter what you believe, I can't give you what you want anymore."

"Why not?"

"Because."

"Because why?" she said and put her hands together in front of her mouth. "Tell me why."

"Please, Lori-Anne," he said. "I can't do this."

"Do what?"

"You cleaned out her room," he said, his face hardening. "It was my sanctuary and you just went ahead and cleared it out. There's nothing left of her in this house. Nothing. It's like she never was. How could you do that?"

"I'm sorry," she said, her heart ripping apart her ribcage. "I just thought . . . you know, I've always been a doer. I just needed to do something, anything. I thought if her things weren't here to remind us, that maybe it would help."

He looked toward the window again.

"I didn't mean to hurt you by cleaning out her room," she said while tears spilled out of her eyes, leaving dark smudges of mascara down her cheeks. "I was just hoping to get you back. I need you. I miss you. I want you."

"What are we now? Without her, what are we? We're nothing. Nothing."

Lori-Anne wiped her cheeks with her fingers. "That's not true. We're still who we were before Nadia."

"No we're not," he said, pounding the top of his desk. "Without Nadia, we're just two people."

"We're two people who once loved each other enough to have a child. We can still love each other without that child."

"I don't think we can. Not after—" Mathieu stood and walked to the window. "Back then we could look forward to having kids. We can't do that now. So what do we look forward to?"

"Each other."

He kept his back to her. "Maybe that's not enough."

"Why can't it be?"

Lori-Anne heard children's screams and laughter waft through the open window, a sound that wilted her heart. A life without Nadia had never been her choice, and she wasn't choosing a life without her husband either. Why couldn't he see her? She was right here. She wasn't going anywhere. She wouldn't abandon him.

"Mathieu, give us a chance."

"I can't."

"Yes you can. You're choosing not to."

He didn't answer.

"You'll never forgive me, will you? You need someone to blame and I'm it. You're giving up on us. You're giving up on me."

"I'm sorry."

"Are you?" she said, her voice cool. "Maybe you didn't take my dad's money, but you're sure taking the easy way out."

"I'm sorry," he said again.

EIGHTEEN

July 2, 2012
9:23 p.m.

L ori-Anne, bag in hand, closed the front door. The rain
had eased off a bit so she didn't get too wet while she
hurried to her car. She put the key in the ignition and
looked back at the house. First Nadia, now her. There were a lot
of endings lately, too many.

She drove off, wondering if her life with Mathieu was really
over.

Minutes later she pulled into her sister-in-law's driveway. She
sat there for a few minutes, unable to get her legs to move. She'd
chosen to come to Nancy's because going to her parents' wasn't
an option after what her father had done. What a mess her life
was. All because of that stupid accident.

"I'm sorry honey," she said in a voice that was no more than
a shaky whisper. "I'm so sorry I got mad at you and grabbed
your phone and took my eyes off the road. I hope you can forgive me."

She felt it in her chest, that tightness that made it difficult to
breathe, and then it rolled up to her shoulders, and it came out

low and quiet, her grieving, like she was afraid to draw attention to herself. Or maybe she felt ashamed, because she'd brought all of this on herself, and Mathieu, and how could she blame him for not being able to forgive her? Like her mother had said, she needed to forgive herself first but at the moment it was pretty damn hard to do.

It was impossible. She'd made so many mistakes over the last three months, beginning with her daughter and then her husband. Maybe she wasn't all that different from her father, needing to control every aspect of her life. He'd lost Brad long ago, when he'd moved all the way to Vancouver to attend university and afterward had settled there, and Cory had been estranged from Samuel since he was a teenage boy and had brought home a boyfriend. And now, because of her own need to control, she'd lost Nadia and Mathieu.

"You raised me well, Dad," she said and slapped the steering wheel. "Damnit!"

The front door opened and Lori-Anne saw Nancy standing in the doorway. She grabbed her bag and headed toward her sister-in-law.

"You're getting all wet," Nancy said. "That bag tells me this isn't exactly a social call."

"My life," Lori-Anne said and followed Nancy into the house, "is a bloody mess."

The two women hugged and then made their way to the living room where they sat beside each other on the black leather couch.

"What's going on?"

"I don't even know where to begin," Lori-Anne said and then over the next fifteen minutes she told Nancy everything.

"Did he actually tell you he wanted a divorce?"

She nodded. "He did. I still can't believe it. I never thought I'd lose my husband. Not like this."

"I can totally relate."

Lori-Anne touched Nancy's arm. "I'm so pathetic, spewing all this on you while you've got your own problems."

"Don't worry about it," Nancy said. "I'm actually doing OK. The kids, especially Nicholas, have been great. Now that I've got my head screwed back on, I'm sort of worried about Caitlin. She's really hurting and I need to spend time with her."

"She's going to be crushed when she hears about Matt and me."

"Let's not tell her right away. Things can still work out."

"I suppose," Lori-Anne said and rubbed her temples.

"Are you OK?"

"You wouldn't have some Tylenol?"

"I have some upstairs in the medicine cabinet. Be right back."

While Nancy ran upstairs, Lori-Anne went to the front window and peeked between the curtains. It was dark now and the road was quiet. No one walked by on the sidewalk. She turned toward the fireplace and saw pictures of Caitlin, Nicholas, Suzie, and Derek on the mantel. There were no pictures of Nancy and Jim.

"Here you go," Nancy said.

Lori-Anne took the pills and cup of water Nancy handed her. "Thanks. Are the kids not here?"

"They should be home soon. I always tell them to be home before dark, but do they listen?"

Lori-Anne put the cup of water on the coffee table and sat down.

"Oh boy! Insert foot in mouth. I'm sorry. I wasn't thinking."

"Don't apologize. Just love them as much as you can, and then love them more," Lori-Anne said and fought oncoming tears. "I've got a case of the waterworks lately."

"I'll join you."

The two women stood in the middle of the living room, tears running down their cheeks. Nancy fetched a box of tissues.

"OK, enough of that," Lori-Anne said. "I need some good news. Come and sit and tell me what's going on in your crazy world."

"Well, I decided that it was best to give Jim his divorce and move on. I didn't want to at first. He's the only man I've ever been with. Isn't that unheard of these days? Anyway, I was really scared when all this happened, you know, having to take care of myself and the kids. That's why I started drinking. But the kids, like I said earlier, they're so great, and they believe in me. Plus they're pretty pissed at their dad."

"I bet," Lori-Anne said. "My brother's an idiot."

Nancy shrugged. "I had some good years with him. We have four great kids. But you know? I'm ready to face life as a single woman. I look forward to it."

"What will you do?"

"I have no idea," Nancy said. "I know Jim will take care of us but I want to do something, get out there. Maybe I'll go back to school and earn a degree."

"You should."

"Yeah, I should. Hang out with the hot young guys."

"Mrs. Robinson," Lori-Anne said.

They both laughed half-heartedly, as if they weren't sure that the moment was right.

"Aunt Lori-Anne! What are you two laughing about?" Caitlin said and closed the front door.

"Oh, nothing," Nancy said. "Just girl talk. Where were you? It's getting late. You know I don't like it when you're out after dark."

"It's summer mom, and I told you I was going to Joanne's," Caitlin said and sat on the loveseat across from them. "So you guys going to tell me what's so funny?"

"We'll embarrass you," Lori-Anne said.

"Oh whatever," Caitlin said. "So why're you here?"

Lori-Anne glanced at Nancy.

"What?" Caitlin said. "Something's going on. Tell me."

"We don't know for sure, honey," Nancy said. "So maybe we should wait until we know more."

Caitlin shot to her feet and came closer. "What's going on?"

Lori-Anne looked up at Caitlin. "Your uncle and I had a really big fight and I needed someone to talk to so I came here."

"You're getting a divorce, aren't you? Just like Mom and Dad."

"Your uncle is just being stupid," Lori-Anne said. "I'm sure things will work out once we've both cooled off."

Caitlin backed away, shaking her head. "No. You can't. You just can't. You can't let it happen. I'm going to go talk to him, he can't do that, I won't let him."

Caitlin rushed upstairs and came back down carrying her backpack.

"What are you doing?" Nancy said.

"I'm going over to talk to him. I packed my PJs so I can sleep there, so don't wait up."

"You can't bike now. It's dark."

"Fine," Caitlin said. "Then Aunt Lori-Anne can drive me."

Lori-Anne reached for her niece. "Sweetie, I'm not going home tonight. I came here to talk to your mom but also to ask if I can crash here. Uncle Mathieu needs some space right now."

"No!" Caitlin said and pulled from Lori-Anne. "I need to talk to him. He can't do this. Nadia wouldn't want this and I don't want it either. Why are the adults in this family so fucking screwed up?"

"That's enough," Nancy said. "I won't have you talk like that. My daughter is not trailer trash."

"Mo-om," Caitlin said in a whiny voice.

Nancy held up a finger. "This isn't your situation. It's your aunt's."

"But—"

"We need to give your uncle some space," Lori-Anne said. "And see what happens. I know you're upset, but right now it's what's best."

"But—"

"Caitlin!" Nancy said. "Your aunt is right. This is her problem, not yours, and you have to respect that. Your uncle needs time to think things through."

Caitlin dropped her backpack and crossed her arms. "I just want to help."

"I know you do," Lori-Anne said. "And I thank you for it. But Uncle Mathieu needs to be left alone. He needs to make some tough decisions."

"How long?" Caitlin said.

"I don't know," Lori-Anne said. "As long as he needs."

"But—"

"No more buts," Nancy said.

"Fine," Caitlin said. She grabbed her bag and climbed, heavy footed, the stairs to her room.

"Poor kid," Lori-Anne said.

"A lot has happened in her life. She's young. Sometimes she acts all grown up but inside she's still my baby girl. I'll go talk to her."

Lori-Anne stopped her. "Just let her sleep on it. Hopefully, things will get better, soon."

Nicholas came in, said hey to his aunt, and disappeared into the kitchen.

"Don't let that carefree attitude fool you," Nancy said with a big smile. "He's really been wonderful since Jim left. Takes care of things around here without being asked. Took care of me a few times that I'm not proud to admit. Maybe now that my life is getting back to normal, so will his."

"Hopefully he's not keeping it all in."

"I had that same worry, but he's always been level-headed," Nancy said. "Come. Let's get you settled for the night."

NINETEEN

July 6, 2012
1:00 p.m.

On Friday July 6, 2012, Flore Delacroix was put to rest. The congregation was much older than it had been for Nadia, and Mathieu noticed that the mood wasn't entirely gloomy, faces weren't pained with grief, and an air of acceptance and hopefulness reigned.

Mathieu reasoned the elderly were used to death, or at least had come to terms with it, and while he could understand that, it didn't give him any reasons to pray. God had taken someone else from him, and how long before He took his grandfather?

Soon they were headed for the cemetery where Father Russo said a last prayer and his grandmother's urn was put into a small shallow grave next to Nadia's. Mathieu moved to the side and watched his grandfather accept condolences. A lot of friends and acquaintances had come to the cemetery and it took nearly an hour before everyone was gone, except for Lori-Anne, her parents, and Nancy and the kids who stood a few feet away.

"You OK, son?" Grandpa said.

"Yeah."

"Your grandmother is in a better place. I'm sure she's quite happy to see Denis again."

"What if there's nothing else, Grandpa?"

"What if there is?"

Mathieu had no response to that.

"Son, we're all here just for a very short time. It's what we do and who we love that make it all worthwhile. See that young lady over there," he said and pointed toward Lori-Anne, "she's the one that matters for you. Let all your anger go and go to her."

"I can't."

"I think you can but you're choosing not to."

Mathieu kicked a small stone. "It doesn't matter."

"Of course it does," Grandpa said. "Look there."

Mathieu looked at Nadia's small headstone. The wording, which Lori-Anne had chosen carefully, was engraved beautifully.

Nadia Bridgette Delacroix

1998 – 2012

Forever Missed

Forever Loved

"You remember the day you brought her home?"

Mathieu felt the eight pounds in his arms as if it were yesterday. He'd stared at her sleeping face it seemed for hours. "I'll never forget."

"That little girl was the outcome of your love for Lori-Anne. You can't tell me that love is gone."

"I don't know, Grandpa." He swatted a mosquito on the back of his neck. "Not everyone is meant to stay with the same person their entire life. You and Grandma were lucky."

Grandpa tipped his fedora and wiped his forehead. "Luck had nothing to do with it. Like every married couple, we had to work at it. You don't think I ever got mad at your grandmother? You don't think she ever got mad at me? Hell, when your dad died and she fell into her own depression, why did I stick around? I could have taken the easy way out and left. But I put my own selfish needs aside and helped her, and you, because I loved you both."

Mathieu squinted at the sun. The day was too beautiful for a funeral. Then again, it fitted his grandmother's outlook on life. To him, she'd always been smiling and happy and he had no recollection that she'd been anything else. He wondered if his grandfather was making it up, her depression, to try to coax him into seeing a doctor.

"Maybe some time apart will help," he said.

Grandpa put his fedora back on. "I hope it does."

"Me too," he said and watched Lori-Anne and her family come up and say a few words to his grandfather and then leave.

"Well, guess we should get going," Grandpa said.

"Just like that?"

"If you know your grandmother, she wouldn't want us to just hang around here and be miserable. She'll be with me no matter where I am. Come on, take me home."

"Sure," Mathieu said and shot one more look at his daughter's tombstone.

Forever missed. Forever loved.

Mathieu tried to swallow but his throat, suddenly parched, had shrivelled to the size of a pea.

TWENTY

July 20, 2012
11:30 a.m.

The ideal child starter bed, as Mathieu described it on his website and brochure, was done. He'd built the original one for Nadia when she was three and over the years it had become a parents' favourite. He liked it because it wasn't too high so kids could get in and out easily, and the built-in drawers were perfect for storing toys or extra clothing.

This one, however, had been difficult to make. He knew it was for a three-year-old girl, and as he worked on it over the last few weeks, he remembered building the original for Nadia, and he'd have to take a break, wait for his hands to stop shaking and his mind to focus. He could see Nadia coming into the workshop and asking him if he was done, her sky-coloured eyes round and bright and full of expectation, and he'd chosen his words carefully so he wouldn't see her crash with disappointment, telling her he was making it extra special just for her so he didn't want to rush and make a mistake. He'd show her what he was working on, and after a few minutes she'd go back in the house and leave him be until the following day.

A routine he'd learned to enjoy, a routine he'd grown to expect, a routine he missed. Nadia had been so predictable, but that's what he'd loved about her when she was younger. He'd known what to expect and he'd known what to do.

He hoped the Kirkpatricks, Brandon and Amie, knew how lucky they were right now. Their little girl, Elissa, was the best thing in their lives right now. There would never be another time for any of them like right now.

He'd called Brandon yesterday to tell him he was done and they could pick up the bed today if that worked for them, and as promised, at exactly 11:30 a.m. they arrived and backed their minivan up the driveway.

Mathieu shook hands with Brandon. "We really appreciate it. We would have understood if you'd had to postpone it a bit more, considering . . ."

Mathieu made a non-committal shrug.

"Is this my new bed?" Elissa said.

Mathieu bent down, feeling his knee complain a bit, but he wanted Elissa to feel that she was important, and he'd learned with Nadia that when they were eye-level, her demeanour was different, less threatened somehow and more open to conversation. "I think that bed has your name written all over it. How does that sound?"

Elissa nodded and clapped her hands.

"Why don't we go take a closer look?"

"Come on, Mommy, Daddy, come see my new bed."

"You must have been a great father," Amie said.

Mathieu put a hand over his chest for a second, an unconscious gesture to calm the ache he felt. "It's pretty easy when they're this young. The real challenge comes later." He paused. "Have a look at the bed and let me know what you think."

Mathieu stood back while they examined his work. Elissa couldn't stop jumping and saying how happy she was and it reminded him of Nadia and how happy she'd been with her first bed.

"It looks fantastic," Brandon said. "You do really nice work. The way you blend walnut and cherry together is incredible. I especially like the carving of the sunrise on the headboard. No one carves anymore. It looks even better than the pictures on your website."

"Elissa loves it, and so do I. Thank you. You've made one little girl very happy," Amie said.

Mathieu smiled. "Then I guess it's a keeper. Let me show you how to take it apart. The cross-boards just sit on the rails so they're easily removed, and it's best to take the drawers out too. The rest of the frame is better left together if possible. It's a bit heavy, but if you have someone to help you, it's much easier than taking it all apart. If you need to take it apart, all you really need is a Phillips screwdriver or drill bit and a ratchet set."

"My dad can help," Brandon said.

"Great. Let's load it up in your van."

"That won't leave any room for Elissa," Amie said.

The Kirkpatricks' looked at Mathieu for a suggestion. "How far away do you live?"

"About twenty minutes. Stittsville."

"Let's put the frame in my truck and I'll follow you."

"That's great," Brandon said. "We'll pay you extra."

"No, it's fine," Mathieu said. "I have to get some supplies anyway."

Mathieu and Brandon put the frame in the back of Mathieu's new truck, and protected it with a couple of thick moving blankets.

"We'll be telling everyone about you," Brandon said.

"I can't ask for better advertising," Mathieu said.

"Is that a matching dresser?" Amie said.

Mathieu turned toward the workshop. Another project that he'd delayed but was almost done. "Not quite the same wood, but I can make one to match the bed."

"I think it would look nice," she said.

"I'd have to look at my order log, but I think I could have one ready by mid-September. Let me know and I can confirm that."

"If you could?" she said, looking at her husband who nodded.

Mathieu went up to his office and returned a few minutes later. "Third week of September. Does that work for you guys?"

After filling the order form, Mathieu got in his truck and followed them to Stittsville. He helped Brandon bring the bed up to Elissa's bedroom, and left shortly after. Seeing Elissa's room had been like stepping back in time, a litter of stuffed animals piled in a corner waiting for a new bed to sit on, an assortment of Barbies stuffed in a clear bin, and posters of Merida from *Brave* on her walls instead of Simba from *Lion King*, which had been Nadia's favourite movie at that age. Elissa's room was so like Nadia's room had been in 2001. Mathieu had felt this pressure in his chest and had needed to escape. Seeing how happy the Kirkpatricks were had brought back memories of better days and left him knowing another piece of him had been hollowed out and crushed.

When he got to the intersection of Carp Road and Stittsville Main Street, he pulled into the McDonald's parking lot and sat there while he calmed down, breathing deep and slow. Outside, the summer sun was a searing dish that mercilessly sucked the water out of him. He thought of going into the fast food outlet to get a drink, but couldn't find the will to do so. The world seemed to bombard him from every side, the mid-day traffic heavy with construction trucks roaring by and sounding way too loud in his ears, a group of teenagers jostling and horsing around as they spilled out of Ronald's House, high on full bellies and sugar-laden drinks, the sweet and strong smell of fresh cut lawn from the adjacent high school yard making his sinuses burn which he knew would lead to a headache.

His mind focused on the sound those kids were making as they walked away, words almost decipherable but not quite, words he could fill in from his own past, words full of nothing but good summer fun.

Mathieu closed his eyes and let the cacophony fill his ears, pulled back to happier times when Nadia and Caitlin played on the swing set in the backyard, their cries of joy and laughter like a gentle caress on his skin. Then he thought of the Kirkpatricks' little girl Elissa, and how she had the same hair colour and eyes as Nadia, and he'd seen a dimple on her right cheek. Nadia had stolen his heart whenever she smiled and her dimple flashed at him. Maybe agreeing to make a dresser for them hadn't been a good idea. It meant he'd probably see Elissa again.

But he didn't want to disappoint her. That would be like disappointing Nadia and he'd hated doing that.

Mathieu started his truck, turned on the A/C, powered up his window, and headed home. He didn't bother to stop for supplies as he'd lost his desire to work. Once in the house, he poured a double whisky and chased it with a beer. He sat at the kitchen table and not for the first time, thought of ending his suffering. Since Lori-Anne had left three weeks ago, he'd functioned mostly in a haze, sleeping as much as he could and only getting up to finish the few orders he had left.

Mathieu poured another double whiskey and chased it with the rest of his beer. That would be lunch and dinner for today. He'd lost ten pounds since Lori-Anne left, never felt like eating. The sinus headache was draining him. He popped a couple of Tylenols and went to Nadia's room. He sat on the unmade bed, stared at the empty closet.

Worthlessness weighed him down like a blanket of lead. No one would miss him if he weren't here. He thought back to Father's Day when he'd gone to the cemetery. Why had Nadia not let him have that accident? It had seemed like the right thing to do.

They could have been reunited.

He could be with her right now.

Mathieu's headache pounded like two angry fists inside his skull and when he stood, a sheet of white spots exploded in front of his eyes. He lost his balance and collapsed on the bed. He grabbed his head in his hands and squeezed, wanting the pain to just go away. He couldn't take it anymore.

It had to stop.

It had to end.

It had to die.

Mathieu stood on legs that could barely support his thinning frame, and stumbled down the hallway to his office. He reached for the phone.

"Grandpa, I can't do this anymore."

 C3 80

Mathieu was sitting on a stool in the garage with the door open, covered in sweat from the beating he'd given the grandfather clock. It now lay smashed against the far wall.

His grandfather had told him not to do anything, that he was on his way, that calling him had been the right thing to do. But Mathieu had needed to do something. If he wasn't going to kill himself, then he'd need to destroy something else.

Pulverizing the grandfather clock had sapped him of energy. He was tired now, too tired to think. Too tired to do anything stupid.

So he just sat there and waited for his grandfather. A car rolled up the driveway and Mathieu watched Grandpa get out of his Buick and walk up to him. When Mathieu stood, his grandfather simply hugged him. They stood like that for a long time, not saying a word.

"It will be OK," Grandpa said after they parted. "Calling me for help was a phone call I'd been hoping to get. It's good. Real good."

Mathieu met his grandfather's gaze for only a second, and looked past him. "I thought destroying the clock would make me feel better."

"Better that than the alternative."

"Lori-Anne is going to be mad at me."

"Let's not worry about that now," Grandpa said and pulled up a three-legged stool, the same one Mathieu had built when he was fourteen. He sat and Mathieu did the same. "So, you think you can't go on anymore?"

"I'm sorry for making you drive out here," he said. "I know you've got your own troubles—"

"There's no one more important than you," Grandpa said and waited until Mathieu looked at him. "You know that, right?"

Mathieu stood and walked around. He grabbed the sledge-hammer he'd left on top of the workbench and put it back in the cupboard where it belonged. "I can't live with this pain, Grandpa. It makes me sick. I can't eat, can't sleep although I can lie in bed all day. I just don't know how to move on. I pushed Lori-Anne away. How did you live through losing both my dad and Aunt Jacqueline? And now Grandma. Please, I don't know if I can live through this." He turned and looked at his grandfather. "I'm afraid."

Grandpa stood and took a couple of steps toward Mathieu. "We're all afraid. It's not easy to live through a tragedy. It takes courage. And you can't do it alone. You've always been a sensitive boy, and I know how much you're hurting. The one person you need is the one you pushed away."

"I don't know what to do."

"Sit down, son."

Mathieu hesitated but when he saw his grandfather insist, he obliged. Grandpa remained standing. "I spent sixty-three years with your grandmother, and she's gone now. It hurts. But not as much as losing your dad did. It was too sudden. We weren't prepared. Sounds kind of strange to say that, but it's true. With your Aunt Jacqueline, we had over a year to get ready so it didn't hurt as much. Doesn't mean we loved her less than your dad, but we'd made our peace with her dying."

"I don't know what you're trying to say."

"Yes, you do. Nadia was taken from you. You weren't prepared."

Mathieu looked confused. "But Lori-Anne was?"

"No, of course not. But she was there when it happened. Maybe it's a bit easier for her because she was able to say goodbye."

"But Nadia died instantly."

"Someone doesn't need to be alive to say goodbye. Maybe you just need to be there when they die. When your grandmother died, I was holding her, I was stroking her hair, I kissed her forehead. I was able to say goodbye."

Mathieu looked at his grandfather. "How is that going to help me? Nadia is gone. I buried her and said goodbye then, but I still don't feel any better."

"You don't have closure."

"Closure is not what I want," he said, his voice rising too quickly. He waited a beat to let his emotions settle. "I just want my daughter back."

Grandpa stood a little taller. "She's not coming back, son."

"That's not helping."

"But it's the truth," Grandpa said. "As hard as it is to accept, Nadia isn't coming back. I'd trade places with her if I could, God knows I've lived long enough, but life doesn't work that way. I know you don't want to hear this, but I'm going to take you to a doctor."

"I don't—"

Grandpa put up his hand to cut him off. "You're the only family I have left and I'm going to do what is right. You're in a world of hurt and someone needs to get you back on the right track."

"But Grandpa—"

"I don't want to hear any more talk of suicide," he said in that tone Mathieu had heard many times while growing up, that tone that said there was no room for wiggle. "You have a whole life ahead of you, and you will see it through. I didn't raise a quitter."

"This isn't some bully I'm running from."

"Yes it is."

"What?"

"Life can be the worst bully in the world," Grandpa said, and pointed a finger at Mathieu. "And you will stand up to that bully."

Mathieu opened his mouth to protest, but his grandfather's demeanour shut him up. The old man could be as unyielding as a wall when he needed to be, but he could also show a lot of love.

"If you'd meant to hurt yourself," Grandpa said, "you wouldn't have called me. On Monday, you're calling your doctor and you're going to tell the nurse you need to come in now. We're going to find you someone who can help."

"OK," Mathieu said in a voice that was small and tired and resigned. "OK."

"Good," Grandpa said. "Now let's clean up this mess."

In silence, Mathieu and his grandfather tidied the garage, put tools away, and swept the glass that littered the garage floor. Clouds rolled in and a gentle rain began to fall, dissipating the hot humid air that had besieged the city for several days.

"Nothing like a good rain to wash away the dirt and rejuvenate life," Grandpa said. "I want you to come home with me. You shouldn't be alone and I can use the help."

"Help for what?"

"Go through your grandmother's stuff," he said. "I'm selling the house and can't bring everything with me."

"You're what?" Mathieu said, holding the broom he was about to hang. "You're selling the house? Why?"

Grandpa rubbed the bridge of his large nose. "It's time for a change. By myself, the house is a lot of upkeep."

Mathieu hung the broom and stood beside his grandfather. "But you've lived in it sixty-three years."

"I need to stare at new walls," Grandpa said and grinned. "I don't need all that space. I found a nice little one-bedroom apartment at the Bridgehaven Manor. Moving in on September first."

"You've already done this? But Grandma just passed away."

Grandpa put a hand on Mathieu's shoulder. "It'll be easier somewhere else. Plus, it will be good for me to socialize with new people. Looking forward to that. Being alone in that house, it just calls for trouble."

"Wow! I never thought you'd ever sell the house."

"Time to let someone else make memories there."

Mathieu gazed out at the falling rain. A thought came to him, quiet and gentle, like a friend. If his grandfather could go on, was it possible for him too? "When does it go up for sale?"

"As soon as I can make it presentable, get rid of clutter. My agent would like to list it Monday so we've got a busy day tomorrow."

"Not a lot of time. You're sure about this?"

"I am," Grandpa said. "It's the right thing to do. I don't want to be alone, and even at my age, change can be good. Your grandmother would agree."

Would Nadia agree that he move on? Would he let himself agree to move on? Could he move on?

"Can you leave your projects for a few days?"

"I don't have much, really. Just this dresser and I still have two weeks. And then I have one more order for September. It's been rather quiet."

"Then go pack a bag and I'll wait in the car," Grandpa said. "New beginnings are waiting for both of us."

TWENTY-ONE

July 29, 2012
7:29 a.m.

athieu thought he'd heard a knock, glanced at the clock on the night table, decided it was too early and he'd imagined the noise. He'd had a horrible sleep, waking almost every hour, disoriented and anxious until it came back to him that he was sleeping in his childhood bed. After the events of yesterday, he wasn't surprised his subconscious had had to psychoanalyze every minute detail. What he wasn't looking forward to was for some doctor or psychologist to do the same.

That wasn't happening right now, so no point dreading it. He turned over and tried to fall back to sleep. But the knock came again and he glared over his shoulder at the bedroom door.

"Get up," Grandpa said.

"It's only seven thirty."

"We're going to the nine o'clock service."

"The what?" Mathieu sat up in bed and rubbed the sleep from his eyes. "You're kidding?"

"I never kid about church. Best way to start Sunday."

Mathieu fell back on the mattress and closed his eyes. Another hour of sleep would be so nice, thirty minutes, ten?

"I can still drag your butt out of bed if I have to," Grandpa said. "I've never missed Sunday mass and I'm not missing it today. Won't hurt you to come along and pray to your daughter and grandmother. Sure your parents won't mind either."

Mathieu had no desire to go to church, today, or ever. "Why don't I just stay here while you go?"

"You're coming," Grandpa said, opening the door and poking his head in. "Think of it as part of your therapy."

Annoyance began to simmer inside his gut. "I'm not in therapy."

"You will be before the end of the week. Remember what I said yesterday. We're getting you some help and there's none better then God's help."

Mathieu glowered at his grandfather but knew better than to argue. He grunted and dragged himself to the shower. Fifteen minutes later, cleaned, shaved, and feeling somewhat alive, he came out of the bathroom. "I have nothing to wear."

Grandpa stepped into the doorway, dressed in khakis and a red collared shirt.

"You're not wearing a suit?"

Grandpa shook his head. "Most people dress fairly casually these days. Some even go in jeans and a t-shirt. God doesn't really care how you dress."

Having left his long pants at home, Mathieu stepped into a pair of shorts and slipped a plain t-shirt over his head, and then he and his grandfather headed off to mass.

C３ ８０

Mathieu hadn't been in Saint-Remi's church in probably twenty years or more. The small parking lot was almost full but he managed to find a spot and pulled his grandfather's Buick into it. He stepped out of the car and took a long look at the old church. Built in the 1960s it had been modern then but looked its age now. He remembered being dragged here every Sunday until he'd decided when he turned eighteen that he wasn't going to attend anymore. The disappointment in his grandparents had almost made him relent, but he was an adult now and could decide what he did or didn't do.

At eighteen, Mathieu had still been angry with God about killing his parents and that feeling had been revived when God had taken his daughter and grandmother. Standing in the parking lot and looking at the church, Mathieu felt his stomach close like a tight fist. His grandfather had saved him yesterday, and Mathieu understood why Grandpa had insisted he come to mass, but it didn't make him a believer.

It didn't make him forgive God.

Mathieu followed his grandfather who said hello and shook hands with people who had known Flore. He overheard words about his grandmother and what a fine woman she'd been. Mathieu thought he recognized some from her funeral but that day had been a bit of a blur, a bitter reminder that God kept taking the people he loved.

At the entrance, the priest, *le curé Albert* as he was introduced by his grandfather, welcomed Mathieu to the parish and invited him to come back again next Sunday. Mathieu smiled and thanked *le curé Albert* but didn't commit to returning. His grandfather had ambushed him into coming and he just wanted to get through the service. He followed Grandpa and they found a couple seats in the second-to-last row on the right side of the church.

Mathieu's gaze drifted to Jesus crucified on the cross.

The fist in his gut clenched a little tighter.

He looked away and didn't see anyone he'd known as a child, or if he did, they'd changed so much he didn't recognize them. His only memory of mass back then was that it was long, boring, and cut into his playing time. How many times had he sat here between his grandparents while some old priest droned on?

Mathieu shifted in his seat. The pews were still as uncomfortable as he remembered. The stagnant air was hot and sticky, barely moving under the three large ceiling fans. He was glad he'd worn shorts.

Le curé Albert came in from the back and the congregation stood. Mathieu, feeling out of his element, copied what his grandfather did. Soon his thoughts wandered to how much work waited for them when they got back to the house. It was just like when he was a kid. Mass was still boring.

But something happened that surprised him: *le curé Albert* didn't speak in a monotone but with cadence and spirit. Mathieu found himself actually listening to the sermon, words that touched the parts of him that he'd been trying to protect, words that explored love and family loss, faith and being tested, words that resonated as if they'd been written to help him heal. He knew the sermon wasn't aimed at him, but whenever *le curé Albert* looked his way, it was like he was speaking just to Mathieu, a tête-à-tête with God. Despite his resistance, Mathieu started to question his anger. He felt ashamed for the pain he'd caused Lori-Anne and embarrassed for the suicide thoughts he'd entertained as his only way out.

After mass, Mathieu waited awhile as his grandfather met more people who knew him and Grandma. The majority of parishioners were older, but there were several young families as well. Maybe this was something that should have played a bigger part in his life, and something that Nadia should have been exposed to. Not that he had any plans of actually coming every Sunday, but—

He'd think about it.

Why not?

As part of his therapy, like Grandpa had said. He could come for a while, until he was better. Maybe.

Finally, Grandpa made his way to the car and they both climbed in.

"*Le curé Albert* wasn't bad," Mathieu said.

"He does have a way with words."

Mathieu turned to his grandfather. "He did seem to. Maybe the new generation of priests are more grounded in the real world."

Grandpa smiled. "That could be. Young people don't want to hear the same old thing they can't relate to. Even old folks. I like him. He's refreshing and your grandmother enjoyed his sermons. Some of the more traditional folks don't like him, but sometimes we need a change."

"How come Grandma's service wasn't here?"

"Most people we know don't speak French."

Mathieu nodded and started the car. "Let's grab something to eat."

"We better just get it to go. We've got a lot of sorting and packing to do."

Mathieu pulled in the first Tim Hortons he saw and went through the drive-thru where he ordered two coffees and three hot breakfast sandwiches. He handed one to his grandfather and wolfed down his two.

"Hungry?" Grandpa said.

Mathieu, mouth full, nodded, then took a sip of coffee. He eased the car into traffic and headed back to his grandfather's home.

"Sure you're doing this?" Mathieu said.

Grandpa got out of the car and stretched. "It's what I need to do."

03 80

Monday morning, under Grandpa's scrutinizing eye, Mathieu made an appointment with his doctor for the next day. Grandpa went with him but waited in the waiting room. Mathieu tiptoed around why he was here until Dr. Steinbach figured it out and after a long talk he prescribed Cymbalta and urged Mathieu to go see Dr. Gilmour.

"So?" Grandpa said once they were outside.

Mathieu held the prescription paper between his fingers, waving it like a white flag in surrender. "I have to get this filled and come back in a month to see how I'm doing."

"Good. And?"

"He gave me the number of a psychologist, a Dr. Melinda Gilmour. He said she's really good at helping people who . . ."

Grandpa gave a reassuring nod. "It's OK son."

"I hope you're right, because nothing feels OK. What if these damn pills don't help or Dr. Gilmour can't help?"

"You love your daughter?"

Mathieu felt scrap metal slicing and cutting as it fell to the bottom of his gut. "What sort of question is that?"

"Put your faith in her and everything will be OK."

Faith wasn't something he had, but if somehow his beautiful daughter could help him come to terms with her death, maybe then he'd start believing in miracles. "I'll give this a try, for Nadia."

Grandpa gave him a gentle slap on the back. "Your grandmother would be pleased."

TWENTY-TWO

Aug 2, 2012
1:23 p.m.

Mathieu arrived a few minutes early for his first counselling session. Dr. Gilmour's office was located on the upper floor of a small plaza at the corner of Broadview and Carling, just beside the medical building where he'd seen the knee specialist all those years ago. He climbed out of his truck and took the stairs to the second floor, room 205, to the right of the stairwell. He grabbed the doorknob, took a deep breath, and entered. There was some ambient music playing from ceiling speakers, barely loud enough to be heard. No one else was in the waiting area and Mathieu was relieved. No point parading his problems in front of a bunch of strangers.

"Mathieu Delacroix for Dr. Gilmour," he said to the young woman behind the counter.

She gave Mathieu a smile that was meant to put him at ease, a smile he was sure she'd perfected over time greeting everyone who came into the office, a smile that was sunny and beautiful but did nothing to chase the anxiety he'd felt all day. "Please fill these out and Dr. Gilmour will be with you in a few minutes."

He took a seat, filled out the forms, and just as he finished, Dr. Gilmour appeared from behind a closed door. She took the forms and led him back to her office. He sank into a plush leather sofa chair while Dr. Gilmour sat at her desk and reviewed his information. When she was done, she pulled her chair around the desk and positioned it closer to where he was sitting. Mathieu retreated further into the couch.

"I thought I'd be lying down," he said, his voice sounding nervous and childish to his ears. "That's how it is in movies."

"I prefer a more relaxed atmosphere where we can discuss comfortably. Can I get you some water, coffee?"

"Water would be nice." His salivary gland had been locked away.

"So, things have been a bit overwhelming lately?"

Mathieu felt the muscles in his face tighten. "That's being kind."

"How would you describe it?"

He took a sip of water. "I'd say my life has gone to hell. Sorry, didn't mean—"

"Don't mince words. Part of dealing with our feelings is to be honest about how we feel. You shouldn't hold anything back, OK?"

Mathieu nodded. "My daughter died in a car crash. My wife was driving."

Dr. Gilmour made notes but didn't say anything.

"And now we've split up."

"So, some major trauma lately."

"And my grandmother, the woman who raised me because my parents died when I was six, just passed away too."

Dr. Gilmour jotted that down too. "How does all that make you feel?"

There is was. He'd been waiting for this part. Isn't that what they always asked in the movies? My daughter is dead. My grandmother is dead. My parents are dead. And my wife left me because I treated her like crap. Woohoo! Let's party!

"How would you feel?"

"Let's concentrate on you for now," she said.

Mathieu stood and paced. Dr. Gilmour looked quite young but he figured the accreditations on her wall affirmed she knew what she was doing. He didn't see any pictures of kids or significant other on her desk. "I loved my daughter . . ."

He covered his eyes but it only made Nadia's image clearer.

"Why don't you sit?"

"I feel like you're looking down at me from your chair."

Dr. Gilmour repositioned the other sofa chair so she would face him, and sat. Now, they'd be eye-level.

After a moment, Mathieu returned to his sofa chair.

"Did you want to tell me about your daughter? What was her name?"

"Nadia. She was fourteen. An only child."

Dr. Gilmour noted that too. "That's a big loss."

"You have no idea." How could he make this stranger understand how hollow he felt inside, like someone, God really, had carved out not just his heart, but his soul? Despair glued his reality. But it was coming apart. "It's not right."

"Tragedies never feel right," she said. "You've lost a lot of people in your life, but losing Nadia is especially difficult for you."

"It's impossible, it's . . ." Sitting in this office where secrets were laid bare, where the truth was finally spoken, where it was OK to show your emotions, Mathieu finally gave in to his grief. "Sorry, I didn't mean to . . . it's just so . . ."

"No, it's quite all right. Letting go is a sign that you're ready to begin the healing process."

He wiped his nose with a tissue. "I don't know if I'm really ready. Just because I cried like a baby doesn't mean anything."

"You may not feel it right at the moment, but I've seen this many times. It's like a purging."

"I'm not much of a believer. My grandfather guilted me into coming here. I don't see how any of this can help. I'm supposed to tell you how I feel and everything will be fine? I don't think so."

"It's normal to doubt the process the first time," she said, "but don't give up on it just yet. Let's give it a month to see if we can make some progress."

He threw the tissue in the trash basket beside him and finished the water bottle.

"You've started taking Cymbalta," she said. "It can take two or three months for the benefits to become noticeable. How are you sleeping?"

"Not great."

"Energy?"

"I've had to force myself to get things done. Helping Grandpa clean out the house drained me, but I still couldn't get a full night's sleep."

"How's your appetite?"

"Lost ten pounds."

She made several notes. "Do try to eat, even small meals, to keep your strength and blood sugar stable. It'll help with your moods."

"I can try."

"You didn't say here on the form, but have you had suicide thoughts?"

He wanted to lie, tell Dr. Gilmour that he'd never think of doing something so stupid, but being dishonest wasn't going to help. He also didn't want to disappoint his family, especially Nadia. "Not since I called my grandfather last Saturday."

"Did you want to tell me about it?"

He fixed his gaze on the empty water bottle in his hands, unscrewed the cap and screwed it back on. "I'd made a bed for this young couple's three-year-old daughter and when they came to pick it up, their little girl looked so much like Nadia at that age, and . . . it just made me miss my daughter that much more, and I just lost it."

"Killing yourself will not bring her back."

"It will stop the pain."

Dr. Gilmour put the end of her pen in her mouth. "What if we can make that pain go away using a different approach?"

"And what if it doesn't work?"

"Nothing is hopeless."

He didn't say anything.

"Tell me one thing about Nadia."

He straightened and his eyes glowed, softening the lines on his face. "She had a dimple on her right cheek. Just the one. And when she smiled, that dimple made me feel so happy and secure, as if it was a warm blanket wrapped around me. It's hard to explain but that's how I felt. And I loved having her sit on my lap while we watched TV, her arms around my neck, the smell of baby shampoo in her hair from her bath. I don't know how many times we watched the *Lion King*, but she could recite every character's lines before they said them."

"Those are the moments you need to hang on to when you feel you can't go on anymore."

"But they make it worse, I miss her even more. I'm never going to share such moments with her ever again. My baby girl is gone." Those last words, the weight of their reality, felt like being left behind at the fair, abandoned.

"What you just described wasn't recent, that Nadia wasn't the one you just lost. You might be holding on to a time that you remember as the best time in your life. Nadia wasn't a baby anymore. She was a teenager," she looked at her notes, "fourteen."

Mathieu didn't say anything.

"Maybe she'd become a handful?"

He simply nodded.

"Do you feel you had some unfinished issues to resolve with Nadia?"

Mathieu leaned back against the sofa chair. "We weren't as close."

"And how did that make you feel?"

He slowly squeezed his right hand around the plastic water bottle, crushing the brittle container. "I wasn't ready."

"Ready?"

"For Nadia to grow up."

"Could that reality be preventing you from moving forward?"

He rubbed his face.

Dr. Gilmour waited.

"You think that's my problem?" he said.

"No. Not entirely. Kids grow up and become independent. That's reality. Some do it in a rebellious way, annihilate the parents, while others continue to develop their relationship with their parents while learning to handle their independence. Sounds like Nadia was a bit rebellious."

"I still loved her."

"A parents' love is the strongest love. No denying. And losing a child is the hardest thing for a parent to go through. Regrets are inevitable. Thankfully, we have our memories but they too can skew what we remember and become a barrier."

"I spent months looking at Nadia's pictures and watching home-movies. My wife, Lori-Anne, didn't understand why I did it. She refused to come into her room, like denying Nadia was gone would make her less dead. I didn't see her way as being any better than mine."

"Denial is one of the five stages of loss and grief. So is depression. Everyone deals with tragedy differently. But at some point, everyone has to reach the last stage, the acceptance stage, so they can move on."

"Accept that Nadia is dead?"

"Yes," she said. "Right now it may seem impossible, but that's where we need to get you to."

"And if we can't?"

Dr. Gilmour folded her hands over her notepad. "You wouldn't have come here, no matter how guilty your grandfather made you feel, unless you were, maybe not ready, but at least wanting to get to that next stage. Problem is you don't know how to get there."

"And you'll get me there?"

She shook her head. "I'll give you the tools you need. You're a carpenter so you understand the importance of having the right tool for the job. That's what we're going to do. Fill your toolbox with the tools you need to get your life back."

"Does it really work?" He couldn't hide the skepticism not just from his voice, but from the disbelief in his eyes.

"Yes, it really does." Dr. Gilmour glanced at her watch. "I think today we've established a foundation to build on. Would you agree?"

"I guess."

Dr. Gilmour stood. "We've made progress. It may not feel that way, but we did."

Mathieu struggled to get out of the chair.

"Will you be staying with your grandfather?"

"I hadn't really thought about it. Why?"

"It might be better if you weren't alone for the time being."

There were still things to clean up at his grandfather's, the yard needed some work, and the garage was full of tools that could be sold. "I'm sure he won't mind the company."

"Good. Here's my card with my home number, just in case you need to talk this weekend. Otherwise I'll see you Tuesday."

Mathieu left the office and closed the door quietly, afraid to destroy the fragile foundation that Dr. Gilmour was so confident they'd established. To him it felt as flimsy as a wooden box put together with hammer and nails instead of a dovetail joint.

TWENTY-THREE

Sept 1, 2012
4:03 p.m.

Mathieu put the last box down in a corner of the apartment, looked around, and turned to his grandfather. "A bit small compared to the house, but it's probably big enough."

"There's everything I need here, a large dining room, a living room to meet people, a nurse station and a chapel. They even have an exercise room and spa. I'll be fine," Grandpa said with a grin that wouldn't quit. He went to the fridge that he'd filled on an earlier trip with food he'd had at the house, and grabbed two beers. "Your Grandma and I had a wonderful life in that house, but it was just a house. Had some good times and some bad times." He took a sip of beer. "You know, I think it was the hard times that brought us closer."

Mathieu drank his beer. "I understand what you're saying."

"Life isn't a fairy tale," Grandpa said. "Happy endings aren't real. Life is tough. But when you're with that special someone, the journey is actually pretty darn good."

"I made so many mistakes."

"There's no shame in admitting you were wrong," Grandpa said. "I've been wrong plenty and apologized to your grandmother plenty more. We make mistakes. It's part of life. Show me a man who doesn't make mistakes and I'll show you a dead man. You don't look like a dead man to me."

Mathieu put his empty bottle on the kitchen counter and went to hook up the television and digital box.

"I appreciate you helping me move," Grandpa said. "And hooking those up for me. My old eyes don't see so good up close. I think I need stronger reading glasses."

Mathieu finished with the TV set and went to stand by his grandfather.

"Give her a call. Go see her."

"I don't have anything new to offer."

"So get something new," Grandpa said. "Listen, you helped me pack and get rid of stuff. It was hard to let go of the things that reminded me of your grandmother. It felt a little bit like I was cheating on her, letting her down."

Mathieu understood that all too well.

"But that was just my silly old man's way of thinking." He took another sip of beer. "I know she's up there in heaven looking after me and telling me to stop being so foolish and to just get rid of what I can't use. There's no point in hanging on to those things. It's my memories that matter. No one can take my memories away, and I can take them wherever I go."

"What's that got to do with me getting something new?"

"Your grandmother is gone and I had to get rid of her things because that's all they were. Lori-Anne got rid of Nadia's things. You still have her memories in your heart, where it counts."

At his lowest point, Mathieu had wanted to end his life. But now, a month into therapy and on medication, his life had settled down, his emotions weren't suffocating him. He didn't need to look at pictures of Nadia for hours and he'd found his woodworking passion again, the dresser he was making for little Elissa Kirkpatrick coming along nicely. He looked forward to seeing her face when she and her parents came to pick it up.

He'd been thinking about Lori-Anne a lot too. He hadn't seen her since his grandmother's funeral, and hadn't spoken to her since the night he asked for a divorce. He had no idea how she was, what she was doing, if she thought of him. The fact that he hadn't seen a lawyer yet told him he really didn't want to end his marriage, but that didn't mean Lori-Anne wanted to stay married to him. He wouldn't blame her if she didn't. What was going to happen between them, he had no idea, but each session with Dr. Gilmour diminished his anger toward Lori-Anne and it was just a matter of time before it disappeared.

"Your wife didn't do anything wrong," Grandpa said, reading his thoughts. "She didn't do anything that requires a divorce."

"I know that now. I didn't before, when it all went bad. I was such an idiot."

Grandpa finished his beer. "You really couldn't help it. Lori-Anne's a smart lady and she knows you weren't yourself. Why do you think she tried so hard to get you to see a doctor? Maybe being apart was a good thing for both of you. It's what you do going forward that matters."

"But why would she want me after what I did?"

"You're a good man," Grandpa said. "We raised you to be loving, compassionate, strong. She saw those qualities in you."

"Not lately."

"No. Not lately. But I'm starting to see a different grandson than I did a few weeks ago, the Mathieu we all know."

"What if she's moved on?"

"Can't pretend to know how this has affected her, but I think I know her fairly well and I'm sure she hasn't given up on you yet." Grandpa looked like a man deep in thought. "You know what makes us men?"

Mathieu shook his head.

"It's not our physical strength," Grandpa said, putting his right hand over his chest. "It's the strength of our heart."

Mathieu shoved his hands in his pockets and found a spot on the far wall to focus on. He'd messed up the best thing that had ever happened to him. Without Lori-Anne, there wouldn't have been a Nadia. Just because he lost his daughter didn't mean he had to lose his wife.

He just needed a little more time, to make sure he was good enough for her, no, not just good enough, but completely devoted to her like he once was.

Because that's what you did when you loved that special someone.

TWENTY-FOUR

Sept 22, 2012
11:30 a.m.

T he first full day of fall was a blast of late summer, the temperature a hot 25C and a humidex of 33C. The fan in the garage did little to make the air cooler and Mathieu's t-shirt clung to him like a second skin. He was cleaning up while waiting for the Kirkpatricks to arrive, hoping they'll be happy with the dresser, which he thought was one of his best.

He'd upped the quality and the care he put into his work for this one as it had become special to him.

Right on time the Kirkpatricks arrived and Mathieu watched as the minivan backed up. Little Elissa came running toward him, her pigtails bouncing off her shoulders and a smile as big as the sun on her face. She stopped in front of him and looked up. "Is my dresser ready?"

Mathieu crouched to remove the child-adult barrier between them and returned a smile that was just as big as hers. "It's right behind me. Want to have a closer look?"

She jumped up and down and clapped her hands. "It's sooooo preeettyyyy."

Little Elissa's innocent wonder made him look at the dresser differently, not from the point-of-view of its maker who could still find flaws but instead from the eyes of a three-year-old. And it was pretty.

"I'm glad you like it."

Elissa took Mathieu's hand. "I love it."

It only lasted a moment, and then she let go of his hand and started opening the drawers one by one, but that innocent gesture, that simple touch, was so powerful, so magical, that it reminded Mathieu of the precious moments he'd shared with Nadia long ago, and as he watched little Elissa and how happy she was, he knew that she had come into his life for a reason. Warmth spread through him, and a smile, a real genuine smile, finally found his lips.

"It's gorgeous," Amie said. "It'll look so nice beside her bed, which by the way, she loves."

"Thank you. It makes me happy that she loves it."

They watched Elissa until she'd opened the last drawer and turned their way.

"Come here, honey," Amie said, "so Daddy and Mr. Delacroix can load the dresser into the van."

"You're not going to bring it to our house like last time?" Elissa said.

"It'll fit in the van," Brandon said. "Mr. Delacroix has work to do."

"Oh," Elissa said. "I wanted him to see how it looks in my room."

"We'll send him a picture on the computer," Amie said. "If that's OK?"

"Can we?" Elissa said.

"Absolutely. My email is on the invoice. I'll look forward to seeing it. I'm sure it'll look just beautiful."

"Yippee!"

Mathieu watched them drive off a few minutes later, thankful he'd taken that order after all. Little Elissa Kirkpatrick, blond pigtails and blue eyes and a smile that was so pure and real it had made him believe that happiness was something not just possible again, but within his grasp.

The smile remained on his face for quite some time.

TWENTY-FIVE

Nov 5, 2012
2:56 p.m.

Mathieu pushed the door open to room 205 like he'd been coming here habitually for years instead of just three months, said hello to Jessie like they were old friends, and grabbed a seat. He was humming a song he'd been hearing on the radio, "Lost in the Echo." The lyrics seemed to summarize the last six months of his life, but they also penetrated that hollow space around his heart and gave him hope. And since little Elissa Kirkpatrick had taken his hand, he was learning to let things go. On that day he had realized how lucky he was, and today, finally, the destination he'd be working so hard to reach had arrived. Not that it was his last day of therapy, far from it, but today he'd decided that it was time to start his life again.

It once seemed as if he'd never get to this goal, especially that day he called his grandfather. He didn't want to think what he would have done if he'd had absolutely no one. And now three months later he felt good, slept well, had gained back eight pounds, and best of all he really enjoyed his work again.

He also didn't agonize over Nadia anymore. He'd had two pictures printed and framed. One he kept in his office and the other on his night table. He'd also finished what Lori-Anne had started, packing the rest of Nadia's room. He wasn't sure what to do with her books and CDs, maybe ask Caitlin if she wanted them, but he hadn't gotten to it yet.

Mathieu heard a noise and turned.

A couple, maybe a few years younger than he, came out of an office, put on their jackets, and left without looking at him. He remembered how embarrassed and ashamed he'd felt coming here too, but now he looked forward to meeting with Dr. Gilmour and taking another step forward.

"Mathieu, come on in."

He followed Dr. Gilmour to her office. He sank into the plush leather chair and wondered, not for the first time, if she had chosen those couches purposely to make her clients feel small, or maybe the comfort of the chair around him was supposed to make him feel safe.

"So," Dr. Gilmour said as she faced him. "How was your weekend?"

"It was good," Mathieu said.

"Last week you'd mentioned you hadn't had any thoughts of suicide for a while. You mentioned September 22 as a real turning point."

"That's the day that little girl, Elissa, changed my life."

"She reminded you of Nadia."

"She did. She was so sweet and happy. They sent me a picture of her sitting on the bed I made for her with the dresser beside it. In her hands she held a piece of paper with very coarse letters that spelled out *thank you*. It actually brought tears to my eyes, but in a good way. Kids at that age are so wonderful," he said.

"But you understand your daughter wasn't three anymore, the memories you'd been holding on to weren't recent."

"Nadia was becoming a young lady. And we were having growing pains. At least, I was. I've come to accept that. When she died, I knew I'd never get her back, that I'd never get the chance to make things better between us. I just wanted to remember when I was her hero."

"It's understandable, to a point. But then it became all consuming, and affected your relationship with Lori-Anne."

"I needed to blame someone."

"Do you still blame her?"

He shook his head. "It was an accident."

"Good. Are you still going to church with your grandfather?"

"Yeah, at first I went because I felt obligated to go with my grandfather now that he's alone. But you know, I have to admit that at night, I often say a little prayer to my family. Unbelievable, isn't it?"

"Sounds like going to mass with your grandfather has had some profound influence on you."

"It hasn't been all bad." He sat a bit straighter. "Some things I still have a hard time believing, and maybe I never will, but I feel lighter when I go, like some burden is taken away. Right now, I'll take that as a good thing."

"You're certainly making progress," she said. "And I think you're on the road to recovery."

"But?"

"It's not unusual to have small relapses. Please keep that in mind," she said. "But it looks like a combination of medication, counselling, and possibly a sprinkle of faith is not a bad recipe."

Mathieu nodded. "It sure seems that way. I have to be honest with you. At first I really didn't believe you'd be able to help. I didn't think anything would. I was powerless. I think that describes how I felt. Maybe people I've lost really are looking after me."

Dr. Gilmour waited.

"Not a bad thing if they are. So now what?"

"I'd like to keep the sessions to once a week for a while longer, and then maybe go to every other week," Dr. Gilmour said. "We can see how that goes. Now, what about Lori-Anne? Are you ready?"

"I miss her. I really do. Maybe she'll tell me to drop dead and not bother her again, but I have to try. I need to apologize and tell her how truly sorry I am, if nothing else."

"So what are you going to do?"

"I don't know," he said and rubbed his thighs. "I haven't seen or spoken to her in four months. Should I ask her out on a date? That just feels so awkward. We have things to sort out before that even has a chance. Maybe just coffee or something."

"You'll need to figure that out," Dr. Gilmour said. "Remember that she's been through a lot also and might not be at the stage you're at now. She might not be ready to reconcile."

"That's my biggest fear."

"I don't think you should fear it, but you should be conscious of it. Even though you've been married twenty years, take it slow. It's like starting over."

"All because I was an ass."

"You were deeply affected by Nadia's death. You were severely depressed. It's a serious chemical imbalance that can ruin lives."

"I just wished I could have stopped myself."

"Don't be too hard on yourself. It's a nasty disease. But it can be treated, as you now know," Dr. Gilmour said. "You did the right thing in the end and your life is getting better. That's what's important."

"I really owe my grandfather a lot," Mathieu said. "He was there for me and didn't give up."

"Having someone like that is a wonderful thing." Dr. Gilmour got up and led him out. "I'll see you next Monday."

Mathieu stepped out into the late autumn afternoon, the distant warmth of the sun a gentle caress on his face. There were so many beautiful yet simple things in life, and he felt blessed to be able to enjoy them. He remembered Dr. Gilmour telling him early on how she was going to give him the tools he needed to get better, and he'd wanted to laugh. He wasn't laughing now.

Dr. Gilmour had delivered on her promise.

And now he had hope.

Hope for a new beginning.

Hope that Lori-Anne will forgive him.

Hope that they'll find love again.

TWENTY-SIX

Nov 6, 2012
10:21 a.m.

L ori-Anne came out of Dr. Galloway's office and trudged to her car, her mind a puddle of panic and bewilderment. The wind bit at her face and neck so she drew her collar up. Her hands ached from the cold and when she pulled her keys out of her purse, they slipped through her fingers and landed at her feet. She looked at them on the ground, like she had no idea how they'd gotten there and didn't have a clue how she'd get them back.

The news had deadened her senses and she couldn't move. She saw people walk around her like there was something wrong with her and they weren't quite sure if it was safe to approach, so they didn't. One little girl asked her mother if the lady was all right and the mother just told her to mind her business and keep walking.

How could this be happening? After everything she'd been through this year, how could this be real? It had to be a mistake. It just had to.

Then something in her brain kicked in, and she bent down and snatched her keys. Her hand shook so badly it took three tries to unlock the car. Once inside, she just sat in the driver's seat and stared out the windshield.

Why her? Why now? Why?

She'd felt soreness and some swelling in her left breast a few weeks ago while showering. She'd googled *how to self-examine for breast cancer* and gotten several hits. She'd followed the five steps outlined at BreastCancer.org. The first time, she'd refused to believe it. She'd waited a week but it hadn't gone away. So she'd made an appointment with her family doctor who had tried to tell her not to jump to conclusions, that the lump could be benign. Her doctor had sent Lori-Anne to see Dr. Galloway, an oncologist, who had performed a biopsy and scheduled a mammogram.

Waiting to hear back had been like being locked in a room and forced to listen to fingernails running down an endless chalkboard. Dr. Galloway had wanted her to come to see him, today, so they could review the results.

She had breast cancer.

Even though she knew cancer was common, she'd never actually known anyone who'd had it. Up until today, it had never touched her personally. No one in her family had ever had cancer. Both sets of grandparents had died of old age. Aunts and uncles, too, as far as she knew. Her parents, even though her dad had aged over the last few months and had done things that were uncharacteristic, seemed healthy for their age. So how could she have cancer? She was young. She felt young. She was too young to get cancer.

This was happening too fast. She needed time to get used to the idea. No! She didn't. She didn't want this to be happening at all.

T1, N0, M0.

Dr. Galloway might as well have been speaking a foreign language. And then he explained how the TNM staging system was used to classify the severity of the cancer. Basically, her cancer hadn't spread to the lymph nodes or other organs. She was a stage one. The tumor was less than two centimetres in diameter, which wasn't considered very big.

"What does that mean?" she said.

"We caught it early," Dr. Galloway said. "We have options. We can perform breast-conserving surgery or a mastectomy, followed by twelve weeks of chemo and five weeks of radiation."

Lori-Anne looked at Dr. Galloway, a brave smile on her face, her hands clutching her purse. She'd come alone, hopeful, not expecting the lump to be cancerous, but now she really wanted someone to hold her hand. Not just anyone. She wanted Mathieu. She really needed him right now.

But he wasn't here.

Maybe she would need to get used to facing this ordeal by herself. Maybe this was her life now, a soon-to-be divorced forty-something woman with breast cancer. Maybe this was her punishment for letting her daughter die.

Mastectomy. Chemo. Radiation.

If those three words in the same sentence didn't weigh in the pit of your stomach like a hundred slimy eels, you were definitely in denial. Lori-Anne did her best to keep her breakfast down.

"I'm sure you have a lot of questions," Dr. Galloway said. "We'll go over the options and see what works best."

"Sure, OK," she said. But nothing was OK. Nothing would ever be OK again. Nothing remotely resembled OK.

How she wished Mathieu was here with her. Not her mom, not Nancy. She wanted her husband. He should be here. He had vowed to be by her side until death do us part. She had never imagined that the death of their daughter would drive them apart. Maybe those vows should be clearer, spelled out, say exactly whose death would do us part.

Dr. Galloway spent the next thirty minutes explaining the different procedures, the benefits and drawbacks of each, and then gave her some pamphlets and websites to look at. It was simply too much information. She couldn't speak, couldn't think, couldn't breathe.

"We'll schedule a surgery date as soon as we can," he said. "I know this is a lot to take in, but we caught it early and your chances are very good. Talk it over with your family, decide what you want to do. If you have any questions, we'll discuss them once we have our date."

Lori-Anne nodded. "Thank you."

Had that conversation actually happened? Had she really been told she had cancer? Had she actually thanked Dr. Galloway? All these questions muddled her mind as she sat in her car and watched people going in and out of the medical building.

She tried to guess who else had gotten horrible news, who else had cancer, who else was going through hell like she was.

But she couldn't tell. She'd expected them to look different somehow, but no one did. They were just people going in and out, some hurried, others strolled as if they had all day. No one came out looking stunned, or crying, or angry.

"I'm too young," she whispered. "How can I have breast cancer? Why do I have cancer? It's not fair."

But she knew cancer didn't play favourites, it didn't care how old or young you were. Kids got cancer, so why couldn't she get it too? Cancer was an equal opportunity bastard.

Lori-Anne ran a shaking hand across her forehead. Hadn't she been through enough over the last six months? She'd done her best to be strong, at times burying her pain or pretending it didn't hurt while she tried to help Mathieu, but none of it had worked.

CANCER.

She hated the fucking word. It sounded vile and left her feeling cold and small and not in control. How could she defeat something she knew nothing about?

God! How she didn't want to face this alone.

⋅⋅⋅

After composing herself, Lori-Anne drove back to work and locked herself in her office. She spent the afternoon researching breast cancer on the websites Dr. Galloway had given her, getting familiar with the possible treatments, and finding forums where cancer survivors talked about their ordeal. The survival rate was very good when the cancer was caught early, as she'd been told. The odds were in her favour.

She would have to tell her boss and take an extended leave of absence. Soon everyone at the office would know. Would they treat her differently? Feel sorry for her? Have pity in their eyes? She didn't want that.

"How am I going to tell Mom?" she said to no one. It was after five and the office was deserted. She should be heading to Nancy's, which was home these days.

How am I going to tell everyone?

Lori-Anne stood in front of her office window and looked down. People were bundled up and walking at a good pace. November in Ottawa could be unpredictable. Yesterday had been warm for this time of year and today was colder than normal. Winter was coming, cold and uncompromising, the season of isolation.

She turned and stared at the top drawer of her desk. It had been months since she'd put it away, tried to forget. Lori-Anne pulled out the picture of her daughter and let her eyes soak up every line, every nuance, every colour that made up the image of the young and beautiful woman Nadia had been becoming. She missed her, their last conversation a moment that continued to haunt her. Maybe if she'd shared this with Mathieu, told him what Nadia had said just before she died, how it gnawed her raw day after day, maybe then he would have understood her reluctance to enter their daughter's room. And maybe then he would have understood why she had to get rid of Nadia's things once she did go into her bedroom.

Lori-Anne put the picture on her desk, grabbed her overcoat, turned off the lights and left. She had to get ready for the fight of her life.

On the way to the elevator, her phone beeped three short times in a row. She froze. That buzzing meant only one person. She pulled her phone out of her coat pocket and read the text.

I know it's been a while. I'd really like to talk. Maybe over coffee? Matt.

Lori-Anne looked around as if she were doing something wrong and hoped no one would catch her doing it. But everyone had gone home a while ago.

She read the text again. She didn't know what to do. She wanted to see him, but why did he want to see her?

He probably had the divorce papers for her to sign. Of course.

Not a good day, she texted back. *Can you just mail me the papers?*

What papers?

I thought you had divorce papers for me to sign.

I guess after four months and what happened last time we spoke to each other, you'd expect that. But no, no papers. I never even met with a lawyer. I've been seeing a counsellor. And going to church.

She put a hand to her mouth.

OMG!

She pressed send before realizing that was such a teenage-girl thing to say.

Yeah, I know, he texted back.

That's great. I'm happy for you.

It's been good. Helping me put things into perspective. Any chance we can meet? I have a lot to tell you. I have so much to apologize for. Please let me at least do that.

Lori-Anne took a few steps toward the elevator and then tracked back. She didn't know what to do. Part of her wanted to see him. No matter how badly he'd hurt her, she wanted to see him. You didn't stop loving someone just because things got bad. But the other part of her, the hurt part, had started to move on without him. Then she remembered how she wished he'd been with her this morning.

OK. Where? When?

Starbucks at the Rideau. Fifteen minutes?

I'll be there.

Thanks.

Lori-Anne took the elevator to the parking garage and got in her car. She could just as easily walk across the bridge to the Rideau Centre, but it was cold and she wasn't dressed for it.

She stopped at the traffic light. Doubts began to creep in. Maybe she should just drive home to Nancy's and text him from there. *I'm not coming.* But the light turned green and before she could change her mind, she headed toward the Rideau Centre.

CB ᙏ

The Starbucks was on the second level, which was actually street level with Rideau Street to the north, beside Joseph's Esthetics & Beauty shop. Mathieu stood just off to the side, watching the escalator in case Lori-Anne came up that way but also kept an eye down the concourse in case she came from the far end of the mall. There was a stream of people rushing by and he did his best not to get in the way.

He glanced at his watch. Twenty minutes already. His shoulders sagged a bit. Maybe she'd changed her mind.

He noticed a young couple, maybe twenty, embracing just in front of the American Eagle Outfitters shop, the boy's hands cupping her bottom. The boy whispered something in the girl's ear, she laughed, and they walked away hand in hand.

Mathieu straightened his shoulders.

He scanned the sea of people, this time noticing a business couple, both dressed in impeccable power suits. The woman was staring away and had her arms crossed in front of her while the man was trying to make a point, his index and thumb together emphasizing whatever it was he was telling her. When she'd had enough, she stormed off and didn't look back.

His shoulders sagged down again. Twenty-three minutes had gone by. She wasn't coming. He'd really hoped that she'd come, but he understood if she'd changed her mind. If he were in her place, he might not have come either.

But then he saw someone about her height and with the same hair colour, her face blocked by a man walking in front of her. Mathieu headed that way, the crowd disappearing, the white noise of hundreds of people talking muffled to a whisper, the smell of Lori-Anne's perfume gently tickling his nostrils.

The glow on his face vanished once he saw that the woman wasn't Lori-Anne.

Mathieu hurried back toward Starbucks, his gaze bouncing off faces, hoping he hadn't missed her coming the other way. He'd spent all day yesterday after leaving Dr. Gilmour's office planning how he would do this, never realizing how difficult it would be to contact his wife—his wife—after all this time. This woman had given him a wonderful child, he knew her intimately, but the separation had made strangers of them and now he wondered if it was too late to start over.

ɠ ʬ

Lori-Anne parked her car three levels down and took the elevator up to the main floor. She stepped out with six other people and moved aside, second-guessing her decision to come. Mathieu had surprised her and at that moment, she'd been feeling alone and scared. But now, well, maybe this wasn't such a good idea.

She glanced at the elevator. It would be easy to just get back in. Pretend he hadn't texted and she hadn't come. Just like that. Wasn't it safer that way? Is that what she really wanted?

She wasn't sure. Too much had happened today already, there were too many threads being pulled, slowly unravelling her life. What if Mathieu was the one thread she should follow?

What if he wasn't?

Lori-Anne pushed aside her doubts and headed toward Starbucks, coming from the far side. She kept her pace slow but steady, mostly because it was crowded for a Tuesday night. In a month's time it would be so crazy in here, overcrowded with Christmas shoppers stressed out to buy, buy, buy.

She stopped and let people go around her. Her lips moved as she silently debated with herself, wondering what she'd say to him. Would it feel normal or strained, like two people seeing one another after years and not knowing what to say? It had only been four months, but ugly hurts marred their separation. Could she forgive and forget? Had counselling really helped? Had he finally accepted Nadia's accident? And what's this about going to church?

What did any of it mean? To be honest, she'd given up. The last sixteen weeks, her mindset had shifted toward starting over. Being with Nancy, who was currently back at university and loving it, had really helped. The two women supported one another, encouraged one another, drew strength from one another.

Sort of silly, but Lori-Anne almost wished Nancy was with her right now. For moral support, and to tell her that she was doing the right thing.

Lori-Anne saw Mathieu. He was walking away, like he was chasing someone. Her stomach tightened, an oily slimy feeling churning and burning, pushing against her bladder. She suddenly felt the urge to go to the bathroom. She turned one way, then another, bumping into a teenager whose boxers showed above the waistband of his skinny jeans. He muttered something that sounded like *watchitlady* and followed it with a strange look, like *eeew* what a freak.

She pulled away from the teenage boy and saw Mathieu standing in front of Starbucks, about forty paces from her. He looked the way she remembered him twenty years ago, handsome and vulnerable, strong and fragile, intense and caring. Could the man she fell in love with really be standing less than fifty feet away, waiting for her, wanting her, needing her?

Lori-Anne straightened, took a deep breath, and walked toward her husband. "Hello, Mathieu."

CB 80

Mathieu turned and forgot to breathe for a moment. He felt himself being pulled into Lori-Anne's light-green eyes and reliving better times, when they were both young and full of passion. When was the last time he'd truly looked into those eyes and felt intense desire rush through him? He'd let familiarity dull that light inside of him, not purposely, just caught in the flow of life, busy with work, busy with Nadia, busy just trying to keep up, every day stealing those moments that they'd once shared and cherished. God! She looked beautiful.

"I didn't think . . . this is so . . . I hope I didn't catch you at a bad time?" he said, his voice thick and uncertain. "I really appreciate you coming."

"I was a bit surprised," she said. "But your text seemed upbeat."

He wanted to hold her. But couldn't. He'd lost that privilege months ago. So they stood there, staring at each other while people went around them.

"Let's get a coffee," he finally said. "Iced Hazelnut Macchiato?"

"That would be great," she said. "And a plain bagel. I haven't eaten all day."

"We could go somewhere else if you want."

She shook her head. "That coffee smells too good."

Mathieu ordered and they found an empty table. Lori-Anne draped her coat on the back of a chair. They sat, saying nothing, staring at one another. Mathieu took a sip of coffee. He couldn't keep his eyes off her. If he could have seen her over the last six months like he was seeing her now, none of this would have happened. They would have faced Nadia's death together instead of fighting and growing apart.

"I . . . I don't know where to start . . . what to say."

"It's OK."

"I know this is probably hard for you," he said.

She tore a piece of bagel and put it in her mouth and chased it with a sip of coffee. "I almost changed my mind a couple of times."

"I'm glad you didn't. Things were pretty bad last time we spoke." He saw her nod. "You have no idea how sorry I am. The way I reacted when you cleaned out some of Nadia's things, the way I accused you of not caring, they way I shut you out. It was all bad. I shouldn't have said nor done those things."

Lori-Anne wrapped her hands around her cup but didn't drink.

"You knew I needed help but I was too stubborn. I should have listened to you."

"You couldn't," she said. "I hoped things would get better, that somehow you'd come to realize what was going on, but I was really just fooling myself. It tore me apart to watch you. I felt so helpless. The more I tried, the more you pushed me away."

"If I could take it all back, make it better, I would."

"It's done," she said. "We can't change it. None of it. All we can do is move forward."

Mathieu glanced at strangers walking by in the concourse. Would that be them soon, strangers to one another? "What does that mean?"

"I don't know," she said, bringing the cup to her lips and taking a sip. "For months I prayed for our marriage to get better, but it didn't. I know we have to move forward, but I don't know how to do that or if we can do that."

"You once said that love would help us through it."

"And you said love isn't always enough."

"I said a lot of stupid things."

Lori-Anne looked away. "You really hurt me."

"I know I did. I've replayed those low moments so many times over the last few weeks, trying to understand why. But there is no why. I was sick, and I hate to use it as an excuse, but I couldn't help it. I don't see any reasons why you'd believe me, or why you'd trust me, but I'm asking you anyway."

"I don't know if—"

"Hear me out, and then you can decide."

She nodded.

"Every time I talked about you to my counsellor, every time I explained to her what an ass I'd been, every time I'd convinced myself that you were better off without me, that longing around my heart just seemed to squeeze harder and harder, like it was trying to push my heart through my ribcage. Giving up without trying, without finding out how you really felt or what you wanted to do, it just didn't feel right. I didn't want to give up without giving it one last chance." He took a couple of deep breaths. "I made you a promise once, and if you'll let me, I'd like to keep it. Please, let me make it up to you. Let me take care of you. You mean the world to me."

Cʒ ɞͻ

Lori-Anne's hands were busy picking at the bagel, crumbs covered her napkin and spilled onto the table. She could tell Mathieu was trying, she saw glimpses of the man she'd fallen in love with, but she wasn't sure if she had the time or the energy to let him back into her life right now. For once she was thinking of herself, of the battle coming, and fixing her marriage, unfortunately, wasn't a priority. Maybe, if all went well, they could try later. She should tell him, because if she didn't, he'd think it was over, but the words wouldn't come.

And she was still afraid to let him back into her heart.

Could she? Would she? When she thought back to the loving and caring man she knew, the answer was easy. But there was that morsel of doubt now, a side of him she hoped never to see again.

"There's something I never told you about the night of the accident."

Mathieu sat a little straighter. "You don't have to."

"I need to," she said. "Maybe if I had when it happened, things might have gone differently. We both know Nadia was going through a tough phase, now that we know she had a crush on a boy explains a lot. Love makes fools of us all."

Mathieu said nothing.

"When I'd finally had enough of her not listening to me the night of the accident, I reached over and—" Lori-Anne tried to swallow. Nadia's last words dried out her throat. "When I finally snatched her phone away, she said to me, in this cold and hateful tone . . . I hate you mom."

Mathieu reached across the table for her hand and she gave it to him. She felt his thumb caress the skin between her thumb and index finger, like he did when they first started dating and they'd walk hand in hand. Like back then, she didn't think he was aware he was doing it and like back then, she was sure he had no clue how his touch ignited these little flutters inside her soul.

"Why didn't you tell me? You've kept this all this time? Maybe I could—"

"No, you wouldn't have."

He hung his head low. "You're probably right. Not the way things were. I'm sorry you had to live with that so long. I'm sure she didn't mean it the way it sounded. She was just mad. She often said stupid things, just to get to us."

"I know," she said and pulled her hand away. "But those are her last words. Her last words to me. To me."

"She loved you."

"I know."

"She was just upset."

"I keep telling myself that."

"You did your best."

"Didn't always feel like it." She grabbed the bagel and tore the rest apart. "If only I could have gotten one more try, you know, to get it right."

"Not sure that was possible. We didn't do much of anything right in her eyes the last few months."

"Yeah," she said and glared at the bagel crumbs. "Do you understand why I couldn't go into her room?"

He nodded. "I might have done the same."

Panic, burning acidic panic, rose in her diaphragm. "I didn't want her to be gone any more than you did, because I wanted her to come out of her room and tell me she hadn't meant it, that she loved me. I needed you to tell me it wasn't my fault, that you loved me."

"But she couldn't and I didn't."

"I needed both of you and had neither." Months of solitude and denial finally let go, black mascara streaking down her cheeks. "I was mad at both of you. I needed both of you. I loved both of you."

"And I failed you," he said. "I'm so sorry. I know these words mean little after all that's happened, but if it's not too late, I'd really like to be there for you now, I want to be there for you."

Lori-Anne had wanted to hear those words so much and now that she had, they fell flat, like unwrapping a gift and finding out it wasn't the diamond ring you were expecting but just some cheap imitation.

"I don't want you to feel like you have to," she said. "Like you feel obligated."

"I know I hurt you and I'm ashamed of it. I don't think I can ever make up for that time. But trust me, I want to be there for you now because I want a life with you, because you're my wife, because I really love you."

"It might be too late."

"I don't think it is, please let me—"

"No, it's not that. Today I found out—" She looked away, a hand covering her mouth. She closed her eyes. Shook her head and then stared at her husband. "Mathieu, I have cancer."

Cʒ ʒᴐ

Mathieu felt his hands turn cold and the coffee on his tongue tasted like metal. The sounds around him were suddenly gone, his vision became blurry, and everything smelled like disinfectant.

"You have cancer? No, it can't be. You're sure?"

She nodded. "Yes. I saw my doctor this morning."

"This morning," he said. "I should have been with you. You could have called me. I would have come."

Lori-Anne played with the bagel crumbs, grinding them to nothing. "We haven't spoken in months. You asked for a divorce."

Mathieu nodded, his eyes filled with regret. "I'm . . . sorry. I was so obsessed with keeping Nadia alive in my mind . . . I screwed up. That's what today was about for me, to let you know how sorry I am for hurting you, and to ask forgiveness. But—"

"I kind of put a damper on that."

"You have cancer. It's not about me or my needs. It's about taking care of you. What did your doctor tell you? What are they going to do?"

"He said we caught it early."

"That's good, right?"

"Yes, chances are good that we can beat it."

"How did you find out? I mean—"

"I felt a lump in my breast a few weeks back."

"So it's breast cancer?"

She nodded. "The left one."

"Are they going to remove it? Is that what they do?"

"They can do a mastectomy," she said, "or I can have the tumor removed and the breast reconstructed."

"Really?" he said. "They can do that?"

"Women get boob jobs all the time," she said, trying to make light of it. "It's probably no big deal for a good plastic surgeon."

"I never thought of it that way," he said. "So it's just in your breast?"

"For now."

"What do you mean?"

"The longer we wait, the higher the chances are that it can spread. We have to move quickly. I need to decide soon which procedure I want."

"You can't do this alone."

"I know."

"I want to take care of you."

"Are you sure?"

"I've never been more sure."

Lori-Anne met his eyes. "It won't be easy. I . . . I could die. Can you handle that possibility? I can't let you back into my heart if you're not—"

"I won't let you down. I will be there, no matter what happens. I have faith that we'll pull through this, together."

"But what if I don't pull through?"

"You have to have faith that you will."

"So much has happened."

"I'll have faith for both of us then. Until you can."

Lori-Anne pressed her lips together, and then smiled a tired smile. "Is my Mathieu back? I'd really like him to be."

"Please, I want you to come home." He took her hands. "Our home where you belong."

Mathieu helped Lori-Anne to her feet and put on her coat. He'd almost lost her once, he wasn't losing her again. She needed him and he was going to be there for her, no matter how difficult it got. He'd made progress over the last few months, things he hadn't believed in, therapy, medication, religion, were slowly changing him. He had a lot going for him, a lot of people looking out for him, and he was going to use their strength and their love to care for the one person that meant the most to him.

Lori-Anne Delacroix.

He had fallen in love with her the moment he'd seen her all those years ago, and seeing her today and being with her made him realize that he had never stopped loving her, he'd just sort of gotten a little lost.

He looked at her and she kissed his cheek.

"Thank you."

"I should be thanking you for giving me this chance," he said. "Now, let's go home and beat this thing."

They started to walk away, Lori-Anne holding on to Mathieu, and all he could think of was that he wanted to grow old with her, he wanted to watch her get wrinkled and grey, he wanted to hear her complain about all her aches and pains, he wanted to hear her breathing as she slept beside him, he wanted to be reminded everyday how damn lucky he was. This beautiful, wonderful woman was his wife and he loved her and their journey together wasn't done yet.

The best part was just beginning.

TWENTY-SEVEN

March 26, 2013
2:01 p.m.

L ori-Anne and Mathieu sat in the car, holding hands. A bouquet of flowers lay across her lap. She turned to him, and smiled.

"You OK?" he said.

"I can do this."

No one else was around. It was a weekday and people were at work. Mathieu stepped out of the car and Lori-Anne waited until he came around to the passenger side to help her out. She wore one of his Ottawa Senators' toques over her hairless head. Now that the chemo was over, she hoped her hair would start to grow back. The bald look wasn't really for her.

The day was overcast and the north wind had some winter bite left in it. A few birds chirped in the distance, the ones that had returned early to welcome back the new season. Spring, a time of renewed hope and possibilities. This year, it was truer than ever.

So much had happened over the last few months. She'd decided to have breast-conserving surgery and breast reconstruction done at the same time. The procedures happened on December 14, and chemo started a week later. Her last treatment was on March 15 and the radiation had started yesterday. Dr Galloway told her things looked really good.

Lori-Anne had been able to lean on Mathieu through the entire process. At night when she couldn't make it to the bathroom in time, he cleaned up the mess she made. He held her when she needed it, and made her laugh when she couldn't take another day of feeling like a train wreck. He loved her the way she remembered, and she'd drawn strength from his love. Just his presence was often enough to help her find that ounce of fight she didn't think she had. Lori-Anne felt he was a big reason for how well things were going.

That, and Nadia. Not a day went by that Lori-Anne didn't say a little prayer to her daughter.

They'd also found out that Samuel was in the early stages of dementia, the news draining Lori-Anne and making her regret cutting him out of her life. Her father wasn't as indestructible as she believed him to be. No one was. She'd lost enough this past year, and forgiving him was easier than staying angry with him.

"Ready?" Mathieu said.

Lori-Anne felt weak and nauseous, but there was no way she wasn't coming today. It was too important. She grabbed Mathieu's arm and they walked through the ankle-deep snow to Nadia's grave.

"How are you doing?" Mathieu said. "Tired?"

"A little."

"We won't be long."

"I'll be fine." A beam of sunshine sliced through the dispersing clouds. "Feels like someone reaching out to us from heaven."

"Small miracles."

She turned to him. "Have I told you I love you?"

"That's a miracle in itself," he said, "one that I'll never take for granted again. I love you too."

Lori-Anne rested her head on Mathieu's shoulder, and they stood in front of Nadia's grave for a few minutes, saying nothing.

C3 80

Mathieu bent down on one knee to put the flowers in front of Nadia's headstone, and then took his place beside Lori-Anne again.

More sun broke through the steel grey clouds and reflected off the snow, making him squint. Spring, or maybe someone, was trying hard to show its presence. Maybe, just maybe, there was more to come after this life. He liked the idea of reuniting with the people he cherished.

"We miss you, honey," he said. "But we're doing okay, your mom and I." He paused. "Do keep an eye on Mom. She could use your help to get better."

He felt a very light squeeze on his arm.

"Even though you're gone," he said, "you've made our lives better. The hurt we felt losing you, well, that's because of how much we love you. Maybe we didn't always show it or say it, but you meant the world to us. You are our proudest moment."

Mathieu heard Lori-Anne's breath catch.

"You okay?"

"I miss her," she said. "If only—"

Mathieu put a finger on her lips. "We promised we wouldn't go there ever again."

"I know, but—"

"No buts," he said. "We had a beautiful daughter who was the best thing to happen to us. She's gone only in body. In our memories and in our hearts she will live with us forever."

Lori-Anne nodded.

"Good," he said. "We have each other. I'm not letting you go. I'll always be there for you."

"I know," she said. "You've been my strength."

"Actually, you've been my strength," he said. "I owe everything I am to you. And Nadia."

Lori-Anne reached up and kissed his cheek.

"Our baby girl is in good hands," he said, looking over the family plot. "We shouldn't worry about her."

"She is with loved ones," Lori-Anne said.

Mathieu put his arm around Lori-Anne. A year had passed since that horrible day. For a while he didn't think he'd be able to go on. Maybe that's what this past year taught him. When he was truly tested, he found out who he was and what mattered. When he really needed to, he found his love, his faith, and his will to survive.

And like his grandfather had said, if you share your life with that special person, it's all worth it.

If nothing else, the past year reminded him that Lori-Anne is worth it.

In his wife's eyes he saw a sadness that he shared and understood, and if he could, he would take her pain away so she could find peace. Wasn't that what truly loving someone was all about? Putting them before you?

"We'll be fine," he said. "I promise."

Mathieu led Lori-Anne back to the car and helped her climb in. He turned and looked toward his family, the space around his broken heart finally feeling like it was becoming whole again.

He got in the car, kissed Lori-Anne on the lips, and took his wife home.

Did you enjoy *It Happened to Us*?

You can make a big difference. Reviews are incredibly powerful in bringing attention to my books and helping other readers decide to take a chance and read them. I'd be extremely grateful if you could take a few minutes to leave your review on your favourite social media site as well as on any of these sites: Amazon, Kobo, Barnes & Noble, Smashwords, and other online book retailers.

Building a relationship with my readers who have decided to take this journey with me is really awesome, and as a thank you for signing-up to my Readers' Group on my website, you'll get a FREE copy of my novella *We Became Us*. You'll only hear from me periodically when I have something to share with you, and I promise never to spam you. You'll be able to unsubscribe from my Readers' Group anytime you want, but I hope you'll stick around because more stories are coming.

Story behind *It Happened to Us*

I wrote *It Happened to Us* in 2009-2010 after my father passed away. This was the third novel I'd written over three years and I felt it was the most complete. Yet, I sat on it because the traditional publishing route had proved impossible in my previous attempts, but something new was also happening in the world of publishing: ebooks were starting to get noticed. I set out to learn all I could about this new possibility, and the learning curve was steep.

In January 2015, after several rewrites and editing, *It Happened to Us* was published.

Then in 2017, I wrote two complementing novellas, *We Became Us* and *Broken Hearts*, and together they form a more complete story.

I hope you enjoy them all.

Excerpt from

WE
BECAME
US

DECEMBER

1991

C hristmas was nineteen days away and expectations were already so high they were nearly impossible to live up to, but Mathieu Delacroix, a first-year student at the University of Ottawa, always kept himself grounded by thinking of his dead parents.

He'd survived a tragic car accident that took the lives of his mom and dad when he was just six years old. Later on, he'd found out that his mother had been pregnant at the time of her death, which always made him wonder what it would have been like to have a brother or sister. Growing up, he'd memorized the definition of an orphan: *a child who has lost both parents through death.*

So by definition of the word, he was an actual orphan.

Parentless.

He'd been raised by his paternal grandparents and had grown to think of them as his parents. Sadly, as time passed, the memory of his actual parents had faded to the point that if it weren't for their picture on his dresser, he wouldn't remember what they'd looked like.

The sound of their voices had long been silenced.

He loved his grandparents. They had done everything parents were supposed to do, and he would forever be grateful, but the one thing that made him feel lonely at times, especially during the festive season, was that he had no siblings. Some of his friends often told him he was lucky, that he didn't need to share anything with anyone, that he didn't have an annoying little brother following him around like a puppy, or had to wait hours to get into the bathroom because his older sister had a date and needed to make herself look *hot!*

These things seemed rather trivial and he doubted they were as horrible as his friends made them seem.

The voice of Professor Halfpenny (oh, there had been plenty of stupid jokes passed around during the first few days of class before everyone had gotten bored and moved on) stopped as the Teaching Assistant, Lori-Anne Weatherly, a fourth-year student, walked briskly to her desk and sat without looking at the professor or anyone else. Mathieu had noticed her absence these last few days and had wondered whether she was sick or simply not coming back.

He'd gone to see Lori-Anne at her after-hours office a couple of times, not because he needed help, but because he'd wanted to see her. He'd pretended he didn't quite understand something that had been covered during class, hoping to ask her if she wanted to go for coffee, but each time she'd seemed uninterested, so he'd bailed on the idea.

But he hadn't given up.

Lori-Anne was a beautiful woman and, like a lot of young men in class, he'd been attracted to her instantly. However, it hadn't taken him long to realize that she was as smart as she was stunning.

A combination that was a little bit intimidating.

Mathieu watched Lori-Anne from the safety of his seat in the third row. There were a couple of girls in front of him so it didn't appear obvious that he was staring at her, but then he caught himself and looked away, not wanting to give off the wrong impression.

And thought of his parents. They were a mystery to him, a memory that existed but had lost most of its reality. His grandparents often shared stories of them but he always felt like they were talking about people that he didn't know.

Strangers.

And yet, he missed them.

Or maybe he missed the *idea* of them.

He knew it was the time of year when families got together. All he had were his grandparents and his Aunt Jacqueline, who had never married. She was a lovely school teacher, had the best laugh he'd ever heard, and lived in Belleville, a little over an hour away, so he didn't see her often.

She would come up for Christmas Eve though, unless driving was bad. He looked forward to having his tiny family together for a few days. Maybe someday he'd be lucky enough to have a family of his own, possibly three or four kids and a wife he adored.

Which brought him back to Lori-Anne.

She seemed off today. Her golden-brown hair, typically worn in a loose ponytail, was a tangled mess, and the circles beneath her eyes reminded Mathieu of someone who hadn't had a good night's sleep in a while.

He also noticed that she wasn't paying attention to Professor Halfpenny at all. Usually she stared at him as if what he was saying was completely new to her, like she hadn't heard his lesson before—probably countless times. But today she was fixated with whatever was on her desk, and she seemed small, like she was trying to make herself invisible.

Suddenly the classroom was so silent that Mathieu could hear someone wheezing behind him. He looked at Professor Halfpenny and saw him looking at Lori-Anne, and the way he was eyeing her didn't seem quite right to Mathieu.

Like . . .

And then he got it.

He might be young, but he'd been in love before and recognized the signs of a couple who'd had a fight, maybe had even broken up.

It made sense now, why she'd been indifferent those times he'd gone to see her. Stupid him, he hadn't even thought that she might be with someone, especially not a professor.

Had he really thought a beautiful girl like her would be single? *Duh!*

But Professor Halfpenny?

The guy had a ring on his finger. Why would she want to be with a guy like that? Could a guy like Mathieu even have a chance?

Mathieu could already hear his grandfather say *you just have to ask*.

C૪ ૪౧

Lori-Anne didn't want to be here, in this room, with Miles, but she'd already missed the last three days and this was the last day of class before exams started next Monday. She wanted to be available in case some students needed her help, no matter how messed up her personal life had become.

On the home front her father kept pressuring her to come and work with him in the family construction business after she graduated next April, so he could groom her to take over the reins once he retired.

How many times had she told her dad that she wasn't interested, that he could just give the job to her older brother Jim? She loved her dad but the thought of being around him every day was simply not something she wanted. She couldn't wait to graduate, find a job, and move out. Good God, she was twenty-three and still living at home.

Enough was enough.

And she couldn't quite her job as a Teaching Assistant, no matter what had happened.

But being stuck inside these four walls with Miles—that is, Professor Halfpenny—was no longer something she looked forward to. Up until a week ago, that is.

What had she been thinking? To get involved with a married man with two kids? His oldest boy was sixteen, closer to her age than Miles himself was. She'd known it was a mistake back in September when she'd fallen for his smooth lines and wanting blue eyes. She'd believed his lies about how his wife neglected him, didn't understand him, didn't want him anymore.

Could she have been more naïve?

It was all her dad's fault. She'd wanted to distance herself from his control so badly that she'd convinced herself that falling for her English professor was her way out. Really? Had she really believed the man would leave his wife of almost twenty years for her? He was forty, nearly old enough to be her father.

She had gone from one father figure to another.

How pathetic.

A good psychologist would have her figured out in one session. Probably less. She had become the clichéd mistress.

She could just *scream*.

Too bad Nancy, Jim's wife, had not finished her degree in psychology. At least then Lori-Anne could have gotten her counselling for free. She loved Nancy like the sister she didn't have. What her sister-in-law saw in her brother was something Lori-Anne had never been able to figure out. To her, he was the annoying older brother who was as much a control freak as their father.

Lori-Anne pulled her shoulders closer, wanting to disappear into her desk, if that was possible. She stared at nothing in front of her, just to avoid looking at Miles. His voice, though . . . his voice was so damn sexy, each word rolling off his tongue like a soft kiss on the back of her neck, and it was all she could do not to run to him and beg him not to end it, to insist that she wouldn't pressure him anymore to leave his wife, to promise that she was going to be the good and quiet mistress that he wanted.

When had she become so weak? So needy?

Just then the entire room felt too quiet, as if everyone had suddenly vanished. But she knew it was just Miles who had stopped talking, and she could feel him looking at her.

Lori-Anne closed her eyes and took several deep breaths. She could feel the weight of her mistakes crush her. This affair had screwed everything up, had completely derailed her plans. She continued to breathe deeply, each breath like a hand pulling the strong woman she'd always been back to the surface, restoring her strength, her common sense, and most of all, her identity.

She was Lori-Anne Weatherly.

When she finally lifted her head, it wasn't Miles that drew her. She simply couldn't look his way. Instead, she scanned the rows in front of her and saw many sympathetic looks, mostly from the female students who seemed to understand, but then her gaze fell on Mathieu Delacroix and she could tell he also understood what was going on. She recalled the few times he'd come to see her after class pretending to need her help, but he was an A-student and didn't need her help. It had flattered her that he might have a bit of a crush on her but she'd been unavailable at the time.

But now that had changed.

Her affair with Miles had been a regrettable lack of judgement and she finally realized that she should distance herself from him as quickly as possible. She was too young and had too much ahead of her to let this indiscretion ruin her life. She had plenty of time to make things right.

She was no one's dirty little secret.

CB ED

Mathieu didn't mean to stare at Lori-Anne but now that he understood that she'd been unavailable and not necessarily uninterested, he found it impossible to take his eyes off of her. Sure he'd had a little crush before, but now he saw her differently, not just as a Teaching Assistant he'd tried to flirt with, but as a woman he wanted to get to know. And the fact that she looked like she'd just crawled out of bed, with no makeup and a tangled mess of hair that had apparently gotten the better of her, didn't scare him off either.

In fact, she couldn't be more beautiful.

And he didn't just think it; it wasn't some teenage boy infatuation. The feeling was real, if not a bit overwhelming.

But he welcomed it. It had been a long time; far too long. Life hadn't always worked out as he'd hoped, but he'd never lost the positive attitude and solid values his grandparents had instilled in him.

And he knew they worried about him as they grew older. His grandmother had often dropped hints that she hoped he would meet a nice young lady someday.

Soon.

He understood her worries. They weren't going to be around forever and she wanted him to have a family of his own. And he wanted that too. Someday.

But he was just twenty-one.

There was time.

And maybe that time was right in front of him. What if Lori-Anne was the one? He didn't want to *put the cart before the horse,* as his grandfather was apt to say, but there was no harm entertaining the idea.

No harm at all.

He could feel the stupid grin on his face get bigger and when he noticed that Lori-Anne was looking right at him, he wanted to dive behind the girls in front of him so that she didn't see the moron he must seem.

But before he could, he saw her smile back.

◌ ∞

Funny how something as simple and innocent as a smile could not only energize a tired soul, but could also chase away what seemed like a lifetime of regrets.

And it felt good.

It really was more than just a smile; it was the latch that released all the locked-up feelings she'd been fighting with these the last few days. She'd made so many mistakes lately but finally Miles Halfpenny was withering away. She had run into his arms in search of vindication, and also to get a break from her father's overbearing expectations, but today she needed neither.

Maybe today was the day her life finally got back on track. She had come into class feeling small, rejected, and beaten, but that sense of dejection was beginning to fade.

Replaced by a feeling of renewal.

Lori-Anne gathered her belongings and walked out on Professor Halfpenny. She didn't utter a word nor did she look at him, and as she pushed through the massive lecture hall doors that led out into the corridor, she knew in her heart that she was doing the right thing, that she was a strong woman and had never really needed Miles Halfpenny at all. As the doors closed behind her, she felt relieved, as if all the doubts she might have had had been left inside with Miles, where they belonged.

At this point she didn't care if she lost her Undergraduate Teaching Assistant position. Becoming a teacher had never been her dream anyway.

Cʒʒ ʒ◌

Mathieu watched Lori-Anne walk briskly across the room and get swallowed by the lecture hall doors that were so large and heavy that they closed with the speed of a turtle. He couldn't figure out what had just happened and he couldn't even begin to understand what any of it meant.

Lori-Anne had smiled back, that's the only thing he knew for certain.

But why?

Had she really meant to?

When he'd lost his parents and had gone to live with his grandparents, he hadn't understood why his parents weren't coming back. Every night for months he'd had terrifying nightmares that woke him screaming and thrashing. His grandmother always came rushing to bring him comfort but he would kick and punch her to get away, shout that he wanted his mommy and daddy, not his grandma. She never backed away, and instead spoke in a very soft and non-threatening voice, a soothing voice full of reassurances and patience and love. She would try to explain that unfortunately his parents couldn't come back; as much as they loved him, they were with God now.

He'd been angry with God for stealing his parents. He'd been just a little boy, a little boy who'd wanted is parents so much that he sometimes wished he were dead with them.

Today was another day that left him wondering what was going on. The older he got, the more he realized how little he understood.

What had just happened now with Lori-Anne?

His grandmother had once told him that not all things in life made sense, that sometimes we just have to accept what is and make the best of it, and often we just have to listen to our heart and follow what it's trying to tell us.

That had made no sense when he was a six-year-old boy who had just lost his parents. But today, her words made sense. His heart was telling him that he should go after Lori-Anne.

So he grabbed his things and left class.

☙ ❧

Lori-Anne's first thought was to go to the office she shared with Miles to grab her things, but then she worried that he might come after her there so she decided to simply go to her car and head home. Right now, the further away she could get from the university and Professor Halfpenny, the better. She knew she was still fragile, and if he came after her and made all sorts of promises, she might fall for his lies again.

And she didn't want to.

She also had to tell her dad to stop pressuring her to join Weatherly Construction. He needed to accept that it wasn't what she wanted, and respect her decision. She was certain Jim would do fine running the company one day (after all, he was a hardass like her dad, so she was pretty damn sure he'd keep everything and everyone in line), but that wasn't the issue. No, the issue was that her dad wanted *her* because he needed her to keep Jim in line, but babysitting her older brother shouldn't be her problem.

Lori-Anne reached her little Volkswagen Golf, tossed her things onto the passenger seat, and headed home.

As she pulled away, she checked her rear-view mirror and thought the boy who came busting out of the same door she'd come out of moments ago looked a lot like Mathieu Delacroix.

A not unpleasant twinkle filled her eyes and a tiny smile pulled the corners of her mouth, but at this very moment she couldn't make time for him.

Hopefully later.

What Lori-Anne needed right now was the comfort and wisdom that could only be found in the person she trusted and valued the most: her mother.

Excerpt from

BROKEN HEARTS

DECEMBER

2011

Thirteen-year-old Nadia Delacroix and her cousin Caitlin Weatherly ogled Spike, the lead singer and guitarist of Teen Spirit, a Nirvana tribute band that was playing up on stage for the school Christmas show.

Spike had the whole Kurt Cobain thing going—the unruly long blond hair, the attempt of two-day-old growth on his baby face, and most of all the angst. He could have been Kurt's son except that Spike had been born in Ottawa, nowhere near Seattle, and his parents were not the famous couple.

This was the last act of the talent show, and the whole crowd was into it, even a few teachers who were drawn back to a time when they were about the same age as the kids and Nirvana was the biggest band on the planet.

Nadia and Caitlin were at the front of the stage, so close they could see the sweat on Spike's face.

"I'm in love!" Nadia shouted.

266 | François Houle

"You and every other girl in school," Caitlin shouted back. "But don't get your hopes up. He's a senior and already has a girlfriend."

"Do you *like* ruining my dreams?"

Caitlin grimaced. "No, but you need to come back to reality, Nad. He doesn't even know you're alive."

"He just smiled at me."

Caitlin rolled her eyes. She loved her cousin, but lately Nadia was being an idiot. It was Spike this and Spike that, as if she and Spike were a couple. Sure the guy was good-looking and Caitlin did her share of staring at him, but she wasn't fanatic like Nadia.

"Or he smiled at his girlfriend who's standing right behind us."

Nadia turned. "I don't see why he likes her. I look better than her."

"Maybe because she's a senior too and they've been dating since grade nine."

"How would *you* know how long they've been dating?"

"Nicholas told me."

"Your brother knows Spike?"

"Not really. Nick's just a junior. He knows Spike but they're not friends."

Nadia appeared deflated.

"And his girlfriend isn't someone you want to mess with," Caitlin added. "She has a reputation for warning girls away, if you get my drift."

"She doesn't scare me."

Caitlin glanced at Spike's girlfriend. She had a nose ring, a bunch of ear piercings, dark spiky hair, dark eyeliner, dark eyeshadow, dark lipstick. She probably had a dark soul to match.

"I wouldn't mess with her," Caitlin repeated.

"Whatever."

The band finished playing *Lithium* and before the last note faded they started *Smells Like Teen Spirit*. The kids screamed and sang almost as loud as the band.

When the show was over, teachers started to usher the kids toward the exit where parents waited to pick them up. It was eleven and getting late.

"There's your dad," Caitlin said.

The girls climbed into the Pathfinder.

"Hey Uncle Mathieu."

"How was the show?" he asked.

When Nadia didn't bother to answer, Caitlin said, "It was good. There was a dance number by grade seven kids that was awesome, and a grade ten theater class did a real funny short sitcom scene. The best was Teen Spirit. They played Nirvana songs."

"Kids still like Nirvana?"

"Yeah," Caitlin said. "They're still pretty cool for an old band."

Mathieu laughed. "Funny how twenty years can turn a fresh new band into something cool from the past. I remember when they were—"

"Can we go home?" Nadia said. "I'm tired."

With a sideways glance at the teen, Mathieu put the SUV in drive and they headed home.

Ȣ ȸ

Nadia and Caitlin were sitting across from each other during lunch the following Monday. They'd texted throughout the weekend but this was their first face-to-face since the awkward drive home Friday night.

"Listen Cait," Nadia said, "I know you like my parents more than yours lately and that they're your aunt and uncle, but trust me, they can be a royal pain in the butt."

"Yeah, well, if you had to live in my house these days you'd be pretty happy with your parents," Caitlin said.

"My mom can be so strict. She's always on me to plan my future."

"My dad won't even let us fart without asking for his permission first."

Nadia had been drinking a Diet Coke and now it all came out of her nose as she burst out laughing.

"Holy crap, that hurts," she said, and wiped her nose with a couple of napkins. "You could have warned me you were going to say that."

"That was too funny."

"I hate you."

"Yeah, back at you."

It was their thing, which meant they were cool again. Nadia knew that things weren't good at home for her cousin, that her Uncle Jim and Aunt Nancy were having issues, but that didn't make her parents saints or anything. They really could be annoying.

Especially her mom. Just because Granddad had been like a dictator when her mom was Nadia's age, it didn't mean she had to be the same too. Her dad was better, most times, and didn't ride her as much about her grades. Sure they were down a bit this year, but it was just grade eight. No biggie.

Mom made it seem like she was heading for a life on the streets.

Right now Nadia had more important things than worrying about what college or university she was going to go to. That was almost five years away.

The one thing that really mattered to her was Spike and how she was going to get him to notice her and dump his stupid bitchy girlfriend.

Maybe she should start posting poetry on her Facebook page. Spike was a musician, he'd probably like that.

"Earth to Nadia," Caitlin repeated for the third time.

"Huh? What?"

"You've not heard a word I said."

"Sorry, I was thinking."

"Let me guess?" Caitlin looked irritated once again. "Spike? Who names their kid Spike anyway?"

"It's not his real name and you know it."

"Then why did he give himself that nickname? It's not really that cool. Kind of dorky."

"You're just jealous."

"Of what? Having a stupid nickname? I don't think so. If you weren't so gaga over him you'd see it's a dumb name."

"I thought you were on my side."

"Side of what?"

"You know. Supporting me with this."

Kids all around them were starting to get up. Lunch break was almost done.

"Nad, there's nothing to support. You've got it in your head that Spike is somehow interested in you. News flash: He's not. Let it go. In a few months he graduates, and unless he becomes some big rock star, you'll probably never see him or hear from him again."

"Not if I become his girlfriend."

"Even if the dude knew you existed, you think your parents would let you date a senior?"

"They wouldn't have to know."

Caitlin put a hand over her face. "Argh! You're being stupid."

"Why? It could happen."

"Seriously?" Caitlin waited for Nadia to say something but her cousin was busy with her smartphone. "Whatever, we've got to get to class."

ༀ ༀ

Caitlin finished showering. She was only one of four girls who bothered to wash after gym class, and if those other girls thought they didn't stink, well they weren't fooling anyone. Thirteen-year-old girls who've been running around for almost an hour didn't exactly smell like a flower garden.

She liked gym, even if she wasn't that athletic. Her brother Nick was the jock, but Caitlin just liked the class because she didn't have to study anything for this. It was basically like a long recess.

Nadia was way better than her at sports. At least, she had been until her boobs had ballooned during last summer. Now she complained about them being in the way and hitting her in the forehead.

Yeah, like a bit dramatic.

Caitlin didn't have that problem. Neither did her sister Suzie or her mom. It didn't bother her . . . much. Okay, maybe a little, but that wasn't the worst thing in the world.

She was worried about her parents getting a divorce. Lately, her mom and dad argued way too much. And there was a lot of yelling. Mom kept making excuses that Dad was just stressed because they were so busy at work and that Granddad was driving Dad hard. Maybe it was true.

And maybe her parents weren't in love anymore.

Her parents wouldn't be the first to split up. Marco's parents had called it quits last year, as had Angeline's. Jonathan was on his second step-mom. He said she was barely older than him.

What caused people who'd been in love to fall out of love? It just seemed that if two people got married and had kids, that they should be together forever.

She didn't see her parents staying together forever. She didn't even know if they were going to make it through Christmas. That would suck so badly.

Merry Christmas dear, oh and by the way your dad and I hate each other and are getting a divorce. Here's a gift to make it easier for you.

Yeah, that would *so* suck.

It seemed like not long ago that Dad would come home and kiss Mom like he hadn't seen her in months, but now they never kissed. Mom had started smoking again, after having quit when Caitlin was little. Caitlin had taken a couple of cigarettes to try, and holy crap had it burned her lungs! And the taste in her mouth had felt worse than morning breath—probably as bad as those people on Survivor who went without brushing their teeth for thirty-nine days.

The thought of that much gunk in her teeth and on her tongue made her want to gag. If she ever went on the show, she'd definitely bring a toothbrush. That was a must.

Anyway, maybe that's why she was annoyed with Nadia. Her cousin was so infatuated—Caitlin loved that word—with Spike and Caitlin knew first-hand that relationships couldn't survive let alone exist when the other person wasn't returning the affection. A relationship without love was like toast without butter—dry and hard to swallow.

Yeah, she liked that one. Maybe she'd shove that one in Nadia's face next time she brought up her love for Spike. She loved her cousin, but the Spike obsession thing was getting on her nerves. Nadia kept showing her the poems she was writing, but in all honesty, they were bad. Not that Caitlin would hurt Nadia's feelings on purpose, but she didn't think her cousin had what it took to write poetry. Even lyrics for songs wouldn't hire Nadia to write them.

Caitlin liked that one too. Maybe *she* should be the one to write poetry. She seemed to have more flair for it than Nadia.

Or maybe she was just as bad.

Didn't matter.

At least she wasn't the one infatuated with Spike.

Caitlin looked at the clock in the change room; she had to hurry. She dried herself, then slipped back into her regular clothes and beat it out of there to fetch her books from her locker for the last class of the day, her favourite.

English.

CȜ Ȝͻ

Nadia didn't particularly care for science. The fact that it was a mandatory part of the curriculum didn't seem fair, since she had no desire to ever become a scientist. Whoever used anything that was taught in this class?

Except maybe geeks.

And she was nothing like those losers. Why did they all look so weird and . . . nerdy? They didn't wear cool clothes, had stupid haircuts, and were so boring to talk to. All they cared about was school and homework and science projects.

Specially the projects.

It's like it was the highlight of their lives to make some twisted science whatever, like they didn't know that being too smart wasn't good at all for your personal life. You'd think that being so smart they'd know that, but when it came to being popular, smart kids were kind of dumb.

She could hear her mom just now, telling her to buckle up and pay attention, that you didn't get anywhere in life without working for it. It was exactly what Granddad said to her all the time—because he still wanted Mom to drop everything and come run his company. But her mom didn't do what her dad asked, so why should she?

Because you're a kid.

That didn't seem fair. Besides, she was a teenager, not a kid. She had rights. It was her life.

"Nadia, please put your phone away," Mrs. Brower said.

"I was just answering my mom."

"Maybe I should send your parents a reminder not to text during school hours."

"I'll tell them."

Nadia saw her teacher look at her dubiously, but she didn't care if Mrs. Bower knew she'd lied. Let her send a note home. Nadia would figure a way to make it seem like her teacher didn't like her, and she was just texting Caitlin back and it was really Caitlin's fault for not obeying school policy.

Will this class ever end?

I'm so bored.

What? A quiz? Like now? Like right now? That's not fair. Mrs. Bower never said anything about a surprise quiz.

The girl in front of her passed down the quiz sheet. Nadia glanced at it and it might as well have been written in German. None of it made sense. Had they actually studied this?

"You have twenty minutes."

Nadia felt the breath of her mother on the back of her neck. She was going to go ballistic when she learned that Nadia got a big fat zero on this quiz; something else her mom was going to be disappointed about. Seemed this year Nadia couldn't do much right. It wasn't her fault, it was these stupid hormones. Everything had changed this past summer: her boobs got huge, her butt got curvy, and it seemed like her brain got smaller.

Like really tiny small.

Nadia stared at the quiz and she wanted to cry. She had no idea how to answer any of the questions. When had they learned this stuff?

She was so grounded.

Like forever.

Connect with François Houle

www.francoisghoule.com

www.facebook.com/francoishouleauthor

Acknowledgments

It's impossible to write without family support, and I'd love to thank my wife and daughter for letting me lock myself in my office night after night and weekend after weekend. I did come out once in a while so they wouldn't forget who I was.

A special thank you to my editor Ellie Barton whose editorial letter was exactly what I needed to steer me in the right direction and help me shape the story into what ended up in your hands.

Most importantly, I want to thank you for coming along on this journey with me. I hope you enjoyed this story as much as I did writing it.

Until next time, take care.

Also by François Houle

About François Houle

François Houle's books can best be described as character-driven stories that explore the importance that love, family, and friends play in helping us get through the many imperfections and challenges that life has to offer. François grew up one of five boys so it's no surprise that family is a strong theme in his books. A lot of his inspiration for his first two novels *It Happened to Us* and *Beautiful Midnight* and his two novellas *We Became Us* and *Broken Hearts* came from the passing of his father in 2005.

François grew up in a small town outside of Montréal, moved to Toronto when he was ten, and currently lives in Ottawa. An avid reader from a young age, he tried to create a comic book when he was twelve, penned hundreds of song lyrics as a teenager, and wrote his first novel in 1985, a sci-fi influenced by the novel *Dune*. Several horror novels followed, and although none of these books will ever be published, they were important in his development as an author.

In 1985, at the age of 22, he graduated from college with a Programmer/Analyst diploma and then went into the ice cream business with his family, owning three Baskin-Robbins franchises for about 6 years. In 1991, he started his IT career which now spans 27 years, and from 2003 – 2017, he was a Certified Professional Résumé Writer and operated a part-time business writing résumés for professionals at all levels.

If you'd like to get your free ebook copy of his novellas *We Became Us* and *Broken Hearts*, and to stay current with what he's working on, please visit his website at: *www.francoishoule.com*.

Fun Facts About Me

1. I'm a big hockey and football fan.
2. I love alternative music. *(The Cure* is my all time favourite band).
3. I enjoy woodworking.

CPSIA information can be obtained
at www.ICGtesting.com
Printed in the USA
BVHW040431071219
565941BV00019B/1643/P